Where the Road Bottoms Out

VICTORIA REDEL

Where the Road

Bottoms Out

a collection of stories

ALFRED A. KNOPF   NEW YORK   1995

THIS IS A BORZOI BOOK
PUBLISHED BY ALFRED A. KNOPF, INC.

Some of the stories in this collection were originally published as follows:
The Alaska Quarterly Review: "China"
The Antioch Review: "Floaters"
Missouri Review: "Service Servic Servi"
The Quarterly: "Cable Work," "In the North House," "Mender of the House and of Other Modest Objects," "Motherland," "My Little Pledge of Us," "Ruby, Darwin, Eurydice," "Soul to Take," "Where the Road Bottoms Out," "Wool"

Library of Congress Cataloging-in-Publication Data

Redel, Victoria.
    Where the road bottoms out : a collection of stories / by Victoria Redel. — 1st ed.
        p.   cm.
    ISBN 0-679-42071-1
    1. Women—Social life and customs—Fiction.
2. Family—Fiction.
I. Title.
PS3568.E3343W48   1995
813'.54—dc20   94-42899
                                                              CIP

Manufactured in the United States of America
First Edition

To my boys—
Jonah and Gabriel—
for the worlds they give to me

All the thanks that are in me to Gordon Lish for teaching me to let every part of the body and heart make noise. And to Jim Traub, always, thanks. Thanks to my father, family, and friends for all their love—in particular to Lynn Grossman, Jenny Temple, and John Beall for their essential help. Finally, thanks to Richard Corum for getting me started.

My deepest appreciation to the Fine Arts Work Center, the Writer's Room, and the National Endowment for the Arts.

Thanks to The Quarterly, The Antioch Review, The Alaska Quarterly Review, *and the* Missouri Review *for their support and publication of some of these stories.*

Contents

Contents

Where the Road Bottoms Out

I t is a mean thing, I know, to tell my mother to think about the pigeoned-in foot that drags on the street between us. It is mean and I am mean and this early-evening street of even lawns and cut-back shrubs seems to wince meanly at my mother and her foot. I know that is wrong, that lawns and shrubs just grow or do not grow, are cut or are left uncut, and know, too, that what I hear at night is not my mother and my father on the other side of our shared wall in some sweet turn of fucking, but, more likely, it is my father helping to roll my mother over, or him at the bottom of her bed, trying to smooth out the snags that my mother says tighten and bunch inside her foot.

"Let's rest," Mother says, in the drifty voice that has come to be her voice. My mother's new voice is another thing that makes me mean, makes me want to lug her an extra haul around the block. The houses we go past going in reverse go: Smoler, Fistigee, Disik, Woolf, Polero, Charles, us. After us is the dead end, the woods, and then the scary woods. Mother hangs on my arm, her whole body twisted to a question. Would my mother want to hear about the jostling train out of this town and how, each week, I have sat so still on that train? Would she want to know about the man I go to and how he rises from the bed and carries me from room to room, this big man with his big legs? The man has mirrors in each of his rooms, but I do not look. I am like my mother; I am all vanity, even down to my shame.

Her foot stutters against the pavement.

"Mother!" I say, wanting her to see how her hand has floated up to stop, palm up, midair. I want her to look at her fingers with the chipped red polish, her sweater buttons misbuttoned, her skirt lopsided, the gnarled, socked foot. I want her to see this and to see in the same glance the trimmed azaleas, the hedges of squared rhododendron, the paired white lilacs. But I can tell that my mother already sees everything and sees nothing on this street, and that all of it is just the street she is walking on.

"Let's rest," Mother says, crumpling one side of her down to the curb and the rest of her, it looks to me, following down in a buckle of gravity. Kids on bikes wheel past and I am surprised that I do not recognize them. All of her is down there now except for where I have a hold, up under her arm.

"You're getting messy," I say. Now we are both looking down, past a heap of sweater and skirt to the smudgy sneaker, which is, I know, something neither of us wants to look at. Shoes, a closet full of shoes, and not just shoes, but good shoes, Milanese, leather soles, T-straps, pumps, spiky-heel shoes, sequiny, crocodiley, illegal shoes, shoes that have never been worn, or worn once and stored in cloth casings—these are my mother, and not the flat and sturdy sneaker with its muddy bow. I look up instead at what makes a yard on this street: the reseeded patches of brown grass, the slate front walks up to doors where anyone might appear, backyards where something is always sizzling. It is what I have loved: the mixed-up smell of this street and the sound of us children street-bound in pajamas for a "last and after this straight to bed" game of four square. But this, I think, is not what Mother wants. Does Mother want the girth of the big man's legs and the way the big man will not let me stop when I say stop? Does my mother want to know that I leave the big man in his bed and go to other parts of my city, where there is a small man and a blind man and two men and stoned men and brothers, or that running down the three flights of stairs I am stopped by an old man whose room is stacked with newspapers and that I kneel just inside his doorway and take the old man inside my mouth? I have done all this and I have done none of this and I am my mother's daughter.

I sit down, beside Mother, on the curb. When she smiles, my mother smiles with only half a face, the other half rumpled, looking like something that has come unpinned. I am on the wrong side of my mother, who, tonight, is not a pretty woman ambling home, and my mother is such a pretty woman in photographs, where she strikes an arabesque on our lawn or sheaths herself demurely in a blanket so that only her cocked face is visible. Tonight my mother is not a woman who could manage any pose, standing on a high heel, with the other leg kicked up in any playful way; she is on this street—all effort, all accident—trying to just get home.

"Come on," I say. "Race you home."

Home is three rests and a spasm away.

Home is a ranch house no longer bordered by the woods and the scary woods, now razed beyond our house for new colonials and Tudors; the houses in that direction going: new family, new family, new family, new family, until our road bottoms out on the Saxon Woods Road.

Our road is the Sycamore Road.

Home is blood-thinning aspirin and a blue and a white and a round pill and where we lie on her bed until some colorless hour when my mother, tongue thick and roamy, will drift to sleep or wake from sleep, shrilling about her cramping foot. This is the home I walk out from each week to ride the train to the city, to the man, to the other men, to the train, and once again back to home.

The foot between us begins to jerk. I walk fast and then faster, as if I could leave the clomping foot behind and take Mother back to where she will stand before her mirror, dressing for dinner, and I will watch the delicacy of Mother's putting-ons—breasts plumped in a brassiere, nylons, poutishy lips she paints red, her leanings. I have undressed and been watched in my undressings, and always, I think, I was thinking how Mother dressed herself, the back of Mother's arms as she latched a strand of beads, the slippy brush of crepe as she stepped into a skirt, the wink as she watched me watching.

"Come on," I say to Mother, who is curbed again, saying, "Honey, will you just rub it a little, honey?" A little is more of this weight, this weighty foot, than I want in my hands, with Mother saying, "There. There. No! Not there," so that what I do not want to do, I do for Mother not right at all. And all I do is so little, with Mother trying to shake her foot, her foot shaking still even after Mother has stopped trying.

Mother's shoelaces have come undone. The laces in my mother's hands seem too long or too short to turn loops for even a child's first tyings. I am determined to make sure Mother sees what she cannot do. And she cannot help but see not just her mangled bows but the slackened side of her face when she tries to paint her mismatched lips or when she turns from the mirror and slurs, "How's this?" How's this? How this is is holding my mother's hands and together tying shoelaces, or finding Mother on the bathroom floor, unsure of how long she's been there. How this is is my father on the other side of our shared wall, saying, "That's the girl."

I prop Mother against a neighbor's tree. I am rough

with her, yanking her sweater straight, pulling up the socks to where they will fall from again. In this early-night air, the lilac branches cast over us, clusters of small white flowers hang close to Mother's face. The kids on their bikes pass, jacked back, riding on one wheel. This night or some night, his big legs will pin me and I will feel the hard spread of his stomach against my back. For the big man, I will brush my face white with powders. I will trim my hairs. I will hold myself open as the big man climbs his whole big self into me and keeps climbing to where he gathers inside of me high on some mossy ledge. In the morning, when I will come—raw-mouthed and fragrant of semen—to lift Mother from her bed, there will be morning pills and juice and the recrimination of dresses with delicate buttons hanging in her closet. I will open my mouth and the big man will step out. In his hands, my mother's foot will untwist, and Mother will let the big man tie her feet into high, cross-strapped sandals. Then it will be Mother in a swoop of his arms—Mother and the man.

"Once," I say to Mother, "I set up a table on this corner and sold your stuff."

Mother laughs or tries, I think, to laugh, the sounds getting snarled on their way out.

"Your father used to like to take me out into the neighbor's backyards. My God, we broke the Poleros' swing," Mother says, standing free of her mooring, then stumbling back, striking the lilac tree, a spray of flowers sifting down. "Oh please, it hurts from laughing," Mother says, and we both look down at the way her foot tangled on its side flops like some caught thing thrown up on shore.

I step back from my mother. "Come on," I say, and wave to the air between us. "Come on," I say, backing more steps backward. Mother looks so small against the lilac's slender trunk. She totters out on her own and Mother does not make even one step before her foot slides out from under her and she is toppling down. "Come on," I say, "you think we have all day?"

But all day is all we have. All day is whatever time of night my mother calls out, calling that she cannot bear pretending to sleep anymore, and I help her down into salt baths, where she closes her eyes and lies so still. Hours, hours, she will stay there until even the cooled water, she claims, rubs terribly against her foot. There will be mornings of turning away from the mirror to dress and her forgetting what she is putting on while she is putting it on. There are the days of my meanness, mean silences cut by my instructional voice saying she must push herself, that today—up and at 'em, hit the deck—we are going past the nest of our streets on a trek she had better be ready for. There is the all day of all days, the breakfast, lunch, and dinner of it, the eggy smear I find on Mother's clothes even when there have been no eggs. Now is the all day of evening, of front-walk lamps snapping on, the electric frizz of garage doors, of scotch on the rocks, of bikes being junked against fences. A car horn sounds.

"They bought anything on that table. I could have

sold everything of yours," I say to Mother, who—I do not want this—has started to cry. Mother's crying looks like her laughing, the one side of her face runny and the other side pinched. I hold out my hand. Mother shakes her head and pulls—yanking, wrangling—herself up until she is up and balanced, somehow, on her own.

Mother walks. She makes her choppy headway past groomed lawns, past houses of grown-away children, past me. Farther ahead, she stops, looks back with a cockeyed face, and I see that Mother has not been waiting for me to say anything. "You, come on," my mother says. I follow. The twisted foot, her foot, trails like a great untallied boon in some grand adventure, where she has quested and prevailed, and is rightfully bearing herself—the damage and the plunder—to home, then onward.

MY LITTLE
PLEDGE OF US

W e were Russia.

We weren't only Russia. We were Bessarabia, which meant we included those small cities and towns, Galatz and Reni, just across the River Prut in Romania. Our grandfather was Egypt. Our mother's papers said Persia. There were months in Constantinople, our great-grandfather Soltanitzky the composer to the sultan. There were certain Belgians. A Polish Mexican arrived and said he was our uncle.

So much of this happened in another language.

In the easy suburban evening, our parents waited for our American disaster. We were schooled in the talk of fires. We knew what should be grabbed. We were taught to recognize the men who would one day walk up our front walk to take candlesticks, a bribe. We knew the smell of gypsies, who would come to take the youngest child.

In our house, everything ran too hot or too cold.

But don't get me wrong. We girls were girls who could ride bikes. We girls ate franks, drank colas, had TV dinners on Sunday nights.

So, of course, please, don't worry, come in.

Come in out of the barbecue evening; step over the potsys marking the hopscotch game, out of range of the bells of the Good Humor truck. Come in through the red curtain to here, where it smells of cooked beets and sour cream, of sorrel and koulibiak. Come in where the vodka is in cups. Don't be shy. We have no time, only generations. Raise a finger, a voice. Chime in. Everyone is speaking, all at once, all in different languages.

Please to the table; of course you will eat.

A spinach pie.

A blintz.

A cabbage soup.

Sha sha.

Speak up. Have more. Have more. Have a spoon or three of the caviar Mattus has smuggled in the bellies of painted nesting dolls. Squish in, among the dead and the living and the children.

Introductions?

That can all come later.

Now it is enough to know that they came with our faces on them. Out of waters, off of boats, onto wharf and land, they came with our long and with our skinny faces, only longer and skinnier, and when they spoke through our bulbed lips, and did not speak our tongue, we shook our heads to say we understood.

Such tales.

So it is said that our great-grandfather knelt on one knee and played a melody so sweet that the sultan leaned over and kissed his head.

So it is said that our mother learned to dance her tarantella from a strumming band of wine-soaked merchants.

So it is said.

It is said, and it is said, and we girls said, *Cithagan yithagou ithagundithagerstithagand mithagee?*

Natured, nurtured, everyone at this table has a fantastic, tortured story.

How will it be told? With a needle and a spoon, it will be told. And it will be told, too, with a mother's waltz and a father's worry coin and with a treasure box where the youngest child has hidden buttons and feathers, the woolly scraps that help her to sleep, the soup spoon and bread crust she will need when the gypsies steal her and she must find her way back home. It will be told secretly, camouflaged, in a mended language made newly of the old, frayed words. It will be spoken in tarnished silver, in a beaten egg and a whisper, and in the shouting all-at-once voices of all the relatives, each claiming the other is dreaming, has it wrong, and that his story, her story, this story is the only story, the one to ward off disaster, the only one that is right.

Ah, gypsies.

Ah, Galatz.

Have a little more herring, no?

BEHIND OUR HOUSE were the woods we called the River Prut, where we girls ran to hide, drifting on layers of damp, rotting leaves, floating over to the edge of the woods to see whether our house was in flames yet, or if the milkman had dragged our mother off in his metal truck.

Was there ever a disaster? Was there ever a time that we were actually called to the front, we three girls, their young recruits, we three girls, already defectors, armed and trained to shoot to kill? If we had killed, what would we have killed? A cossack? A postman? The slow boy who lived down the block? Our mother? Our father?

In the woody River Prut, we stashed away rations that we claimed would hold us for a week. We worked our way through a box of crackers in an afternoon and buried the empty carton. My sister said we would learn to survive on air. She gave each one of us one of Mama's cigarettes. We foraged for acorns. We chewed sticks. We made plans for a rendezvous at the mouth, where the River Prut meets the Danube.

We were, always, finally, their only disaster.

Our mother standing at the back door screaming our names.

Bloody noses.

A stitched eye.

Our papa waiting up for us when we tottered in, smoky, from parties we swore were chaperoned.

We were always teetering, on the verge of looking too much like whatever was out there.

"You are not American," our father said when we marched with the school band.

"You are not American," our father said when a sister came downstairs frosted-lipped, wearing a black armband.

"What do you think you are?" our father asked.

For enough of the time, we girls were like everybody else—kids hanging from trees, kids with forks and stiff-legged dolls, kids looking for other kids we could tease for being different or dumb, some kid my sister tricked into eating soap powder, the slow boy we bribed to strip almost naked, anyone we could master or make stick out so that we did not stick out quite as much.

From the banks of the River Prut, we watched our house. We saw how our family must look to the others on our street. What was inside looked suspicious, our uncle in shirtsleeves, waving a wooden spoon, our mother and father rushing at each other, playing bull-fight with a table spread. We could hear our father shouting, "Do you think I am the tzar" as he went through rooms. It was not what our father said but how he said it, his rhythms all wrong, and the way he switched midsentence into another of his languages or stopped at a window and stared out as if he were seeing our street for the first time.

Mostly though, even in daytime, the shades of our house were drawn. They were foreign inside, shadows stretched funny by light, and we could not recognize exactly who was who or what lived inside of that house.

We could see our mother, the strained look on her face when she called, "Girls." She stood in the doorway in a sheer wrap skirt and tights. "Girls," she repeated, getting softer with a fear we could watch overtake her body, so that soon she was not so much walking through our yard as creeping through it, whispering our names.

"Don't go back!" our sister said.

"Girls," our mother trembled close to us.

Our oldest sister grabbed our wrists.

"Don't even breathe," our sister said.

We thought about the air we had eaten. It should hold us.

We pretended our mother was not our mother.

It burned where our sister's nails dug into our skin.

"Please," our mother whispered, bargaining with the soldiers we knew she believed had come for us.

It looked terrible—our mother hunching through the yard in her chiffon skirt. She stumbled and muttered. The ground was muddy with spring. We could have touched her, come out to her or brought her into our hideout on the banks of the River Prut. We let her stay out there, wheeling and crawling through the yard, calling out for her children until doors opened. Other parents cradling babies—hands protectively on the necks of the older ones—came out for a look.

Our mother ran in for our father.

Our oldest sister said she deserved the worry, the way our mother dressed in slippers that laced at her ankles. Our sister asked, did we see any other mother who drove through town in leotards, a camel hair jacket draped over her shoulders?

Our oldest sister started singing. "Oh beautiful," she sang. She walked up to the front door, singing.

We followed.

"For purple mountains," we sang together.

Our parents came to the door. Our father said something to our mother in a language we did not understand. She pulled in, standing close to him. They looked past us to the other neighbors watching our family from their front steps.

"Are you through?" our father asked, though it sounded like *true*.

The wind was thick behind us, racketing in over the woody River Prut.

"Come in, girls," our mother said, flaring her nostrils once.

We went in.

The bowls of kasha were still burning-hot.

N o w i s the time.

It might as well be the time, I think, to relax, get

cozy, take off the shoes if you have not already, and make our introductions. Mama, the mother; Papa, the father, Nana Gusta with her sisters and her brothers, and her husband, our grandfather, and his father, and, perhaps, too, the drunk sultan himself with his thirst for music, and Uncle Marie with his good head of hair and his sour wives and their curdled offspring, and even here, too, is Fokine, nephew of the famous Mr. Fokine, and Madame Swoboda, and Esperanza, one of the flamenco twins from Seville, and Irina Fedovata, and the Polish uncle from Mexico that we called Monsieur Max.

Shake hands.

Kiss cheeks—both cheeks.

Do not worry that you cannot remember the one from the other. Stay a little while; have a bowl of Fokine's bouillabaisse, and you will start to simmer in dialects of languages that you have never learned. There are, of course, others—a cousin who arrived by mail, floated in when my parents forgot themselves and left a door slightly ajar. There were cakes named for aunts who never showed up, and there was an extra sister we believed our mother kept in the old bassinet just in case the youngest child never found her way back home.

Us girls? We are the daughters one, two, and four, the third our mother's fifth-month loss. We are called for always all at once. We come downstairs together, a flock, all flutter and hem, hand-me-downs handed down twice. We are the Anderson sisters, shoulder to shoulder to shoulder, singing, "Daisy, Daisy, answer my question true. . . ." Myrna, Louise, Greta, Bette, and Marilyn, we name ourselves straight out of Hollywood. Our names change with the marquee each week.

Seen but not heard, napkins bunchy with bread and lox, we are off to resupply our stash on the River Prut.

We will be back.

In the meantime, try the pirogi.

OUR MOTHER rode through town in her tights and chiffon wrap skirt, a camel hair jacket draped over her shoulders, the pink slippers ribboned to her feet. Rumor was she had danced with the Bolshoi and for a season with the Ballet Russe de Monte Carlo.

"That girl—not one, but three left feet." Mama laughed and flicked her lit cigarettes onto trim lawns.

The town police waited for our mother. They liked to pull her over, stand at the window and ask her to step outside, "For just a moment, please." Our mother went Frenchie on us for the town police, everything Z-ish and high-rolling R's, her chiffon dance skirt melting in the headlights. She had a kick to her, up on tiptoes, arched and ready for a cancan. We watched the policeman light a cigarette for our mother. She dipped, swayed, gave a little curtsey. We saw the taut line between her shoulders, her readiness to take off and run. They took their time each time—warnings, radio checks, rules explained so slowly that when our mother got back in the car, she said, "All the same, those guards, *les idiots*. Take me home, girls." And she would pull off, smoking out just a bit too fast.

The Russians had nothing good to say about one another. They were always fighting, our mother and Fokine, about shrimp or Fokine's famous uncle, Mr. Fokine, or our electric stove, which Fokine said was impossible and made true bouillabaisse impossible, or our mother saying what did an old Russian know from bouillabaisse, having never been anywhere closer to Marseille than a bowl of borscht.

The house smelled fishy.

Bass heads glanced up out of pots. There were legs on the counter. Grunt and eel leaned, scaled and clean, on the cutting board.

And there were always other Russians in our kitchen, saying other no-good things to one another. There were sudden bursts of silence. They watched one another with slandering eyes.

The kitchen reeked of garlic.

In our house, there was no grace. There were split shells on the table. There was wine. There was Fokine polishing over our polish. There were more fights among the Russians. There was a mazurka and a polonaise. There was rum. There were cries of Bolshevik. There were stains on the linen. There was an aria from Monsieur Max, who fell in love with Esperanza, the elder flamenco twin from Seville. There was the youngest child napping in our papa's lap, waking up enough to say, "I am not sleepy." There were dishes in the sink and dishes on the table and an open bottle of cognac and our papa carrying us one by one up to our beds to tuck us—God willing—in for the night.

Outside, at intersections, with their oaths and eager badges, they waited.

They would wait all night if they had to.

They would pledge themselves ready for what they knew had already crossed the border, had infiltrated, assimilated, weakened the dollar.

They would wait in the dark till it came.

They would flip a switch, pin it in spotlight.

They would cruise the streets of our town, listening to the electric wires.

They would get out the dogs.

They would make it walk the yellow line.

They would watch for lapses, look it in the eye, warn it, ticket it.

They would dismantle it.

They would make it hoist the flag.

They would keep it out.

They would wait all night to keep it out.

They would maintain the order.

Inside, in our house, the sultan—glutted, exhausted, arbitrary as ever—kissed each of our traveled foreheads, closed his one good eye, and, for at least this night, kept the assassins out.

*   *   *

MONSIEUR MAX sat outside on a plastic lawn chaise and waited for the Mexican wind that he said passed through our woods.

"That's my Oaxaca, girls," said our uncle, closing his eyes.

We sat behind him at the edge of the woods. Monsieur Max said that out of the woods was coming the Mexican wind, and up the street were coming the armies of Europe.

It was gummy in our yard, the road filmy with heat.

"Oh, yes," said Max. "Here it comes, girls."

We closed our eyes most of the way, kept him a flickery thing, a bulge and sag in the grass.

We could hear kids down the street. They were a motley after-dinner band, brothers straggling behind brothers, sisters, any kid who wasn't inside or off anywhere better, wandering to the corner, looking for other kids who had wandered out, stringing together chase or war or red rover red rover, or just sitting on the curb waiting for another kid who might have a better idea or just any idea at all.

Monsieur Max said there were bandits in these woods and, fierce and cruel as a Mexican bandit was, we should hide under their wool serapes when the armies of Europe landed on our street.

"Among enemies," our uncle said, "choose your friends."

We could hear them down the street. We could hear that the teams were uneven.

It blued with shadow by the woods where we sat behind Monsieur Max.

"Under their serapes, there is always something—a tortilla, a chipped knife, a bottle to fill with wind for when they flee their country," he said.

He stood up to turn his chair and sat back down.

"Remember, a bandit," our uncle said, "is not so different—like a Polish soldier—that same hollow knock."

He stood up to turn his chair and sat back down.

The game was growing; we could hear it, a mailbox base for safety, someone screaming, "That's not fair," screaming, "Yes," screaming and screaming and screaming until that was, we knew, the game—kids screaming out of bushes, through flower beds, tagging and bombing, tagged and bombed, and now we could hear the mothers out screaming, "Right now!" and "Your father!" and "I mean it!" until they were all gone and the street was so quiet with quiet and dark with the first dark of night.

Monsieur Max said, "There it is, my Valladolid."

We thought we felt it then, the wind, whatever, something in that heat that came through us. We shut our eyes and waited for more.

"Y O U A R E not American," our father said.

He said it, it seemed to us, the way we heard other fathers tell their children not to run out into the street. He said it to us as if the worst had already happened, the way we knew those other fathers knew that there is always a child lurching off a curb, lunging after a stray ball and getting hit.

PAPA CALLED us in from evening street games to look at our books.

"All wrong," he said.

It was, we said, the way they wanted it done.

There was, Papa said, the problem of the numbers. There was the problem of the straightness of rows. There was, our father said, the entire problem of American teachers, who were, he said, hardly teaching anything but a poorness of all habit that might prove to be needed.

We loved them one and all, our teachers with their crisp blouses and blue grade books. Oh, to her blond flip, and after Christmas the diamond ring that Miss Skilken held up to the light. We loved the nurse's cot, where we rolled the thermometer under our tongues. Oh, to color-coded readers, stories of girls and boys out on picnics, the mother with her pleated skirt at the open door. We loved the shop teacher with his jigsaw and belt sander and Mrs. Herman, who read us the news and cried for the hungry children on the other side of the world.

"It will be needed," Papa said. Our father paced the floor, his money belt strapped under his shirt. "And what is all this?" he asked, waving our compositions.

Oh, too, to the under-desk minutes where we practiced waiting for the Russian bomb.

Our father said the teachers listened—a giveaway vowel, a lapse into any language.

We were the Russias. Any explosion was ours. We were tongue-tied, students of the way our teachers spoke, a Boston *R* we brought home, announcing at the table, "Miss Brenner says that's not true."

Papa turned with his sharp look. "I'll show you true."

"All too much," he said, "and too much against America." He blew into the backs of his fingers. "So much opinion? Who are you, the president?" He jiggled his belt, feeling for coins that would pay his way across borders, buy us new names.

We rewrote our compositions while he blew hard into his fingers again to keep—despite his squandered, lost children—what little he had hoarded of luck.

BUT TOO MUCH TALK without nothing! Not so much this as a blintz or a kugel. Not a nothing little sweet? Not a little burek stuffed with spinach and sweet cheese? Not even a tea, the leaves at the bottom forever spelling out *doom*?

Come, come with us. We will sneak away from the table, down the stairs to the basement, where the costumes Nana sews for Mama's ballet are kept.

There were Chinese courtesans, snowflakes, brocade dresses for Cinderella's nasty sisters, bolts of toile and crepe, sequins tacked and stacks of crowns, garlands, the Sugarplum Fairy's tutu, a tutu for each season hung upside down on hangers from the pipes in our basement, where we girls went to light matches and smoke our mother's cigarettes.

Our hands were our mother's hands, her cigarettes put to our mouths, or held ashy at a distance until the ashes dropped. The ashes always dropped. Our legs were ashy and seared where we tested one another, burning the faint hairs down to skin. Our skin was our mother's skin, traversed, foreign, each of us girls a country she crept through to come to bring us forth.

We could hear them through the ceiling, rattling in the pipes, our father counting his stacks of coins, making money belts for each of us, planning and replanning routes out of town, towns to go to, countries where someone else was already living with our name. We could hear Mother opening the back door, asking Father, "Where are the girls?"

We were right there below them, lighting books of matches.

They were never out of sound, the scuffle of feet above us mapping their worries. Their feet seemed slow to us. These were the easy feet to catch, walking predictable turns through rooms, heavy feet, easy to catch up with or run from. We were getting ready to make the run. We stuck matches together, watched them fuse and burn out. We burned our nails and the soles of our feet. We put on the wolf's costume and consumed the swan. We put on the swan's costume and never became the prince's bride. We blew smoke rings in the crotch of Sleeping Beauty. We woke as Sleeping Beauty, torched the castle, and went back to sleep. We woke into the fifteenth century in the burning city of Bern, filled our wooden buckets, and prayed.

We woke in our basement, in our house, on our same street, to the smell of tart apple and brandy and brown sugar in the skillet. We woke tired and weak of foot.

There was crème fraîche on the table.

Spoons in every bowl.

We hurried to eat more than our share.

THE RIVER PRUT flooded. Leaves covered our yard.

Our father said, "Look at us."

We looked almost like every other American family out for Saturday chores—raking, piling leaves to burn. We were all out, even Fokine in his gray suit, picking up leaves one by one. Mother called out orders. We were to get under the rosebushes and up on the rosebushes, where leaves had spun up and stuck on the thorns. The thorns made our hands bleedy and we wiped the blood on the legs of our pants. Monsieur Max stood up from his plastic lawn chair and called out to the brutal winds of Chiapas that he said tore through our woods. It was, declared Monsieur Max, like the love he loved for Esperanza, something to make

29

a man sing. We heard our father singing songs in languages with notes we could not imitate.

"Only in America," said our father.

The piles of leaves toppled and fell, and we girls fell, too, our parents scattering, falling after us, trying to save us from drowning in the River Prut.

WE OFFER our youngest sister for a look at the slow boy scrawling her name with his dick piss. We will double with the Dutch for titty for his father's cigarettes, and more, too, about where our parents have buried arms, and the thing we swear to him we have seen a bandit do to a boy with a bandit's teeth. We could, it feels, keep talking, and we do, telling the boy how to say *fuck* in Pogo Pogo, how we have seen a man charm a snake down his throat, how our uncle has killed a soldier just with words. The eldest is our talker, walking around the slow boy in fast circles until, grinding and turning after her, he trips against the road curb. We take him roughly. We speak in Crocodile and Bulgarian. She tells the slow boy that there are places for a boy like him. "Just look!" She points at his wadded pants. "You're dead." We leave him, scraped, road pebbles stuck bloody to his knees. We leave him, pants down.

We walk home.

We are spies and counterspies.

We are starlets hiding bombs in the spangle of dresses.

They are hiding out in that house, waiting for the soldier and the milkman with his metal truck.

We are running.

Here we come.

LISTEN. . . . You can hear the sultan's dreams when he takes his night sleep by day at our dinner table. The sultan always sleeps by day, fighting Turks in his empire. He tosses, wipes tears from his one good eye on our tablecloth, rises crusty-eyed and hungry when we are called to eat.

Watch. . . . He will not eat from his own plate, not with a fork or with his hands, not until we are all done and the plates are bones and chewed stems and the cabbage we girls spread to the china's far rim. Not until then and then some. The sultan starts with our mother's plate, sucking at the blued empty shells she has stacked, using an end of bread to sop up juice of spinach and garlic from our father's plate, and, over our plates, he winks at us, his mouth stuffed full of all that we girls have wasted.

We were always, the sultan said, in his dreams, wielding great swords. We were true armsmen, beheading without a second thought when the sultan cried out for a head. The sultan said we showed our family's refined taste, catching with a free, gloved hand and never letting a severed head just drop.

But to listen into his dreams, we let his empires fall.

What burned by whose hand where? What woods

are these? The scorched pot? The soup all gone? Where stirred the wind? The Prut, we girls knew, the Danube turned and running inland? A bag of shells? A cigarette? The polished gleam off Fokine's shoes? The tutus aflame? The flames flared out the window like a red flag? What did they see—the slow boy standing on Monsieur Max's lawn chair, screaming *fuck* in Pogo Pogo, the fathers in a huddle behind him? Did they come in the night or by day, the milkman in his metal truck? Did they ride off with the pretty sister whooping, "Take me!"? Or with the prettier sisters, did they kiss and steal into the woods? Whose woods? I think I know. Every house became a secret language. Everything on fire. But nothing burned.

The sultan sighed in his sleep. He called out for us in the names he had for us, and you could hear in the pause between his cries that we girls, his darlings, were traitors, ministering to him so tenderly from a poisoned cup.

WE HAD no accent.

Every language they spoke in that house was a secret language, a code we were always on the verge of breaking.

We spoke English.

We have walked into rooms into far cities and felt at home in the cluck and warble of what we could not understand.

We understand so little. What we do not understand pulses, clots familiarly inside. A worried thread we pull. The frayed woolly edge of a child's blanket.

We have had our children.

We have wandered into Russian beauty shops and, under the facialist's puffy hands and gossip's tongue, fallen fast asleep. We wake to the fighting of Romanian cocks. We feel a wind and hear its Mexican heat.

Our sister sleeps in a pinstripe suit.

Our sister has the messy scrawl of a poet.

Our sister is a mother.

We wake into the disaster of another calm day.

We wake again.

She wakes from a dream of her father, who is not sleeping. He walks in her dream through the halls, stopping at doorways, counting heads. She takes her money belt down to the market and buys her future long. She finds her daughter squatting over a mirror, trying to see up to her heart.

Today is July Fourth.

Please come to our houses. We will feed you a little something, a glass of pale wine. Our doors, we leave them open. We douse charcoal with lighter fluid. We light matches. We have no accents. We eat burgers with catsup, dogs with mustard.

We hear of fleeing, the ones who come on boats.

What a pack of liars is this Russia!

Do you think our father saved a single one? The *patria*. The *patria*.

We gather with the others to watch fireworks.

One sister writes, "It is the Fourth of July." One sister holds a son in her lap.

He says, "Boom."

One sister watches for interest rates to plunge.

They are gone, Monsieur Max and our mother's chiffon skirt.

The money belts are tied up in treasury bills and bonds.

It is America. We are America.

The house is a house that looks like every other house, the River Prut a straggly tangle of trees, our mama, our papa—a mother and father we watch age into the common fretting of the old.

Cithagan   yithagou   ithagundithagerstithagand mithagee?

My sisters say I have it all wrong. I leave out what is important.

We speak such good English.

I leave out Amelia Wanderling and Paul Logaurcia, who danced the part of the prince. I have not said enough about Uncle Marie's good head of hair. Have I said *containment*? Have I said how we held our hands to our hearts and pledged ourselves, how we are sisters who let nothing burn?

There are seconds on burgers, if you are still hungry.

We live, all of us, in the same city, on the same bus line, close to the freeway. We read with a tribal heart about cities in ruin.

They say there are no gypsies.

I have not said Akerman.

The band starts to play. The crowd cheers.

The sultan closes his one good eye when the band starts to play. He listens. The sultan drifts, with a wheeze and a God bless America, into dreamless sleep.

My sisters say there is no sultan.

Drink up. It is the Fourth of July. This is my America.

I have got it all wrong.

A Day in the Park

*T*hey would bury all of her if she let them, and she has let them on days when the sand is permissibly warm and it feels to her like it could do her some good. But even in these coasting days, she is keeping a sort of vigil, waiting for when— and it always does happen—she is tired or light-headed and has to lie down on a shaded bench and the boys take off, blasting fast out of her sight.

But of all days, she thinks this is to be the best of all the days, finding omens in everything, like the nutty smell that she has never smelled in the park before, like her not having had a single woozy moment since she first woke to this best day. Her littlest boy, she sees is an omen, too, dumping truckloads of sand over her legs and shouting out, "Cave in!" in his best worker-man's shout. Or the tag game that springs up, where she is safety base, and the boys run off, and when they come running back to touch her, she is still right there—that, she is sure, is an omen, too.

Whole mornings pass when the boys will hole up in hideouts for resupply and target practice. Then, "Enemy! Enemy!" and across from where she is resting, she hears it is one of her own and she watches him scan benches, his eyes skimming over the West Indian, the Filipino, the Irish nannies barricaded in by loaded-down strollers. "Enemy," he shouts. "Enemy," and then more quietly, "Mom? Are you there, Mom?"

These days, good days, she is everywhere: there on the bench and here in the sandbox and coming upon them in forts, where they are squeezed together, limbs so mixed up that it looks to her like there are more of her boys than she knows there really are. They do not look up at her, or, looking up at her, she sees surprise on their faces and wishes she had not looked.

"Mom," her littlest says, pouncing on home base and going nose-to-nose with her. "Pretend," he says, "pretend you eat me up."

Then she, that shaggy sand beast, pops up at once, eating him in every kind of way, saying in her evilest, beastiest voice, "What a delicious morsel of boy. Such delicious deliciousness," and the bigger boy jumping on her so that the mother must eat him limb by limb, and, in every kind of way, she feels herself for once actually ravenous, lucky with hunger.

*   *   *

A Day in the Park

A DESERT SQUALL. Her big boy announces that they have already lost twenty men. "We must eat and fight on," he declares, brandishing his sandwich with a captain's certainty. The boys are watching her to see if she is eating and she knows it, managing her food slowly, wedging the bready globs into a ridge along her gums. Trying to swallow, a dry yellow feeling crowds at the back of her throat.

"There are wolves, too," her little one says, "and turtles."

"No turtles," shouts the captain. "Anyway, you are out."

"Am not. Right, Mom?" asks her littlest.

"Dead!" pronounces the captain.

The mother knows it is her turn. Her boys, those watchful sentries, have seen, she knows, that this best day is starting to get away from her.

They are watchers these days, finding each new mark when she comes home, or she finds them standing outside her shower door, saying, "Mom, that looks like railroad track." Suddenly at dinner, the little boy is asking, "Mom, do cells nap, too?" Now she tells herself that she must rally, give the troops a show, stand up against the gusts and save her littlest from a desert's bone-bleaching grave. Her arms move in an oversized front crawl and she braves on, despite the heavy, toppling winds. "I've got you now," says the mother, dragging him in a cross-chest carry, cradling him in her arms and getting her big captain boy to help as they resuscitate their little sand boy with loud, smoochy, peanutty kisses that keep going a little too long after his shrieking has turned gulpy and thick.

They have played their way into the center of the park. They are out where she does not want to be, with the other mothers and nannies able to look up at any minute. She looks up, sees a woman has sat down on her bench. The woman is bent over, gurgling into a baby carriage. She feels her boys in her arms, frisky, their legs kicking at the air.

"Mom," they say, wiggling free of her arms, "just go sit down."

THE AIR is filtered golden despite the rain and blue where the leafy shadows bend over the jungle gym, and everyone, she sees, has left the park. She thinks she should round them up, her boys who are ponying back and forth across the asphalt, but the truth is, it is easier to just sit in this easy quiet, pull the bandanna off, let the rain get to her scalp, and wait for the boys to ride themselves back.

The boys have stopped over by the far fence. They step in place, brushing their feet in the dirt, dust clouding around their ankles, and she is amazed how suddenly they really look like horses, shy horses, she thinks, or horses waiting for something, like maybe for young boys with sugared palms to come and lean on the fence.

They knock against each other.

The rain is light, hardly even a drizzle.

A Day in the Park

In comes the bowlegged man who comes to sweep and rake the park. The boys follow, galloping behind the man in a kind of procession past the mother. She can see MAINTENANCE scripted across his heart in green thread. She sees the boys have stopped at the sandbox to watch the man do his work. He is serious and solemn and delicate with his rake. The mother sees that the boys have the serious look of boys watching men work. She is glad for it—though for what exactly, she is not sure—maybe for the way her boys stand watching, pails and action figures dangling in their hands, and for the man, for him she is glad, too, that the boys watch and the mother can see that some of his seriousness is a kind of gladness, too, like when he shows the boys the serrated-edge bottle tops and shards of plastic whatevers, and she can see the boys lean in thrilled and frightened at all that is hidden in the sand. But also, too, she is glad just to have the boys there—at a distance, in plain view. The boys harness themselves to the man's cart, pulling it behind him on his rounds. She sees how they guard his rake and his broom while the maintenance man un-twists the twisted-up swing seats and pulls wrappers and cans out from the turtle tunnel and sets each of the seesaws down in the same direction. They stand at at-tention after he has taken back his rake and his broom and are there still standing after the maintenance man has made his way out of the park, his strong body swinging above the effort of his bowed legs.

Then the boys are climbing her legs, saying, "Mom, don't you even know it is raining, Mom?"

* * *

WHERE THE MOTHER steers the boys is not toward home, but deeper into the park. They are tired, she can see that, the way their sneakers trip and they seem to walk pitched forward and slouched backward at the same time. One path to another path, and then she takes them off paths altogether.

Off the paths, it is cool. The mother holds up a branch and the boys pass under.

"Mom?" says the younger boy.

The brush is thick with vines and stickers. She points, and the boys look frightened that she is only pointing out rocks and bark and places where the little light that is left in the day strikes a branch or a single leaf. The boys have stopped talking more or less, or only every once in a while to ask again, "Where are we going?" She does not tell them where they are going. She is busy looking for what she is looking for, some-place, she realizes now, that she has been seeing all day just on the fringe of all else that she has seen.

She crawls in under a low hang of branches. Poking out her head and taking one look at her wet, bedrag-gled boys, she says, "It's raining out there."

"Mom," says her little boy, "can we go home?"

"Come on," says the bigger boy, turning in a full circle.

She takes their hands, guiding them in under the branches, where the ground is mossy and even what pine needles there are are in such thick layers that they feel mostly soft and only a little bit needlish. The mother bunches the pine needles into three pillows and lays the boys down where she can feel the tensed length of each of her boys pressed against her on either side of her.

She starts talking, handing over to the boys gluey sticks, sheets of mica, holding clumps of dirt under their noses.

"Taste it," she says. "It tastes so dirty."

"Mom, let's go home," her little one says.

She answers by flipping over to her stomach so that she can get her hands stroking both boys' heads. They toss and fling a leg over her and say, "Mom?" while she goes again and then again through the loop of songs she sings to them every night.

"Isn't it something?" says the mother, though by now she hears the grunty breathing of her boys in their first sleep.

"I'm telling you," she says, her cheek settling on a patch of moss, "it really is."

After the boys have settled deeper into their sleeping, she finds herself listening to their breathing getting slow and slower, so that she is moved to poke a little at the boys till they mumble or startle up from sleep, and she says, "Yes, yes, it's okay," and helps shush the boys back down to sleep.

The boys roll close to her and she can feel that a chill has come into them.

She gets up—crawling over the boys—and squats, hooking her heels on a root that gnarls up from the ground.

THE BOYS have squirreled their way to each other, settling so still now, holding each other, the one boy's body like an outline of what the other boy is growing toward. Nights, the mother has wandered into their room and watched them adrift in their own beds, legs hanging off a mattress, a head grounded under a pillow, or whole bodies spun loose, pointing in the wrong direction. And sure, she has come to them in some unknown hour with glasses of water and medicine in teaspoons, or carried them to the toilet and aimed their risen penises into the bowl. She has also waked to find herself—how long has she been there?—kneeling by a bed, touching a boy, worrying the thready cotton of pajamas.

She starts with what is around her—small sticks, pine needles, matted leaves she finds at one corner of their den. She brings back larger sticks and mud from her forays—always within earshot—and she gathers fresh leaves, too, stripping them from branches, a woody smell opening around her.

She lays what she has gathered on thickly, but even so, she is surprised at how little it takes. She piles on twigs, branches, reaching back to patch where the leaves have already slipped off a foot. A foot, a knee, the bony splice of a hip, bones that have been splinted, the zipper scar from some year's snowsuit, not one in twenty fingers left uncovered as the mother works her way up, covering them, now a shoulder, now padding extra thick where they shift beneath her hands. Sticks snap beneath the weight of the earth the mother has begun packing. She finds herself thinking of the man with MAINTENANCE scripted across his heart, coming as he must to clear brush from the overgrown thickets. She thinks of the faint *cha* as his rake enters the leaves. She is heaping the leaves. She is smoothing the dirt. How round it feels to her, a great belly to touch, and she feels something move beneath her hand—what is it? An elbow? A fist? The curled bodies turning in sleep, working their way down?

Somewhere, out there, she thinks she can hear footsteps—no, hooves.

She places leaves on their faces, leaf by leaf so that she will not wake them. They toss their heads, leaves scattering, and she pats them, quieting them with one hand while she covers them with the other. In the morning, the park will fill, mothers and nannies and maybe even a stayed-at-home daddy settling on benches, the swaddled and the bottle drinkers in their laps. Out there, beyond the shaded benches, the shaggy, shaggy, big and bigger boys are swaggering, rocketing.

Hear them cry, "Enemy."

She lies down. She stretches, her body fitted around the mound that is her children. And then, it is only then, at last, that there is rest for the rest of her night.

FLOATERS

*A*fternoons, we stayed poolside when there was a pool, or we stayed in our room, taking turns in the tub, or all of us girls together overflowed the tub while our daddy did business on the hotel bed.

Our daddy's business was town to town.

In the last town, before the last town we had been to, our daddy was in the business of trust—glossy booklets with charts, information that zigzagged in bold and bolder letters. There were trends. But it was Daddy—he made you want to buy, which was no real feat, he said, since everyone out there, he said, was ready to give their money to the first Joe who thought to ask.

We had our business, too, mostly treasure and ransom—and a synchronized swim routine that was particularly hard to practice on rainy days when we were all of us together in the tub. Our business, our daddy said, was to get smart, and so we worked, penning soapy letters on each other's backs, and so, also, on each other's backs we made maps, complete with X marks the spot, dashing and dotting along until we knew it was recess time, and then we played Marco Polo in the pool just for fun.

This is how it was—around doors safely left ajar, through louvered shades—we mostly seeing our daddy in pieces, a shirtsleeve rolled up, boxer shorts frayed, a leg on a turned-down bedspread, a voice announcing, "Good afternoon. This is Mr. Dan. Would this be the lady of the house?" Daddy was everything, but never a Mr. Joe. He was Mr. Polowski in a town where the business was family plots, Mr. Bob Deep when it came to selling water. "Abe Schneider here," our daddy said, offering hot tips in securities and bonds. Our daddy preferred working that way, he said, businesses with no bulky inventory to strap to the car roof, and with an office, he said, where a chambermaid comes in to change the sheets and towels every day of the week.

You could tell a good day's work by the creakings of the hotel bed, our daddy getting himself so worked up with work that he would start bouncing a bit on the saggy mattress, the springs making metally sounds; and us girls, hearing the bed, got worked up, too, with synchronized tub kicks and with one of us starting up a splash fight so that sooner or later one of us would be soap-in-the-eyes crying and there would be Daddy's voice—his "I mean business" voice—saying, "Girls,

girls, for the millionth time, do I have to ask you to let a man get a day's work done?"

BUT A STAY-IN-PLACE couple of weeks, that's what this time it had been.

It did not matter how many times us girls dripped through the room; Daddy was always there on the bed, with the bedspread still neat from where we had helped our daddy turn it down because, he said, "You never know what's been there before you."

In the first days, he was still thumbing the phone book, looking up long enough to say, "Will you please get yourself out of that damp suit, honey," and going back to whatever mostly wasn't in the phone books.

He was Mr. O'Farrell then. His business, fire.

It was supposed to be a sure thing, O'Farrell's fire thing, our daddy said, what with weather that had given not so much as even a squirt, he said, let alone a shower, for months and the trees and shrubs looking like October and the grass around the hotel all brown except for where it was gone bald from the local rules on running sprinklers.

The hotel pool, at least, was still being filtered. We were deep in the days of Junior Olympics. We cannon-balled and dove and did relay races, then stood on the pool's steps to receive our medals, which we accepted as an honor for our nation with our hands blazed over our hearts. The pool was kidney-shaped, and so we would argue over the good side. There were ties and tiebreakers. There were false starts, disqualifications, interviews. We, each one of us, sooner or later won the gold.

It was this way the afternoons went by us. One of us was always making forays to the lobby vending machines and sneaking soft drinks and packaged crackers past the NO FOOD BEYOND THIS POINT sign, past the unattended lifeguard chair, to where the rest of us waited in the shallow end for all the energy-boosting, officially-approved-by-the-Olympic-Committee snacks. By the time the afternoon was evening, we were soggy, waterlogged, raisin-toed old ladies. Stretched out on plastic pool chairs, we were a family of winners, that was for sure, girls who could make their daddy proud of girls.

And it was sometime, some early evening with the sun pinned low in the sky, that we went home to Daddy. We pulled ourselves up and walked—striped backs and legs—back to the hotel room, where we found him sitting on the bed, flipping lighted matches into a filled-up ashtray. On the bed was the phone book, or what was left of the phone book, most of the pages ripped out and balled and torched in the ashtray to a heap of ash.

That night, we were in the tub before he had a chance to say the first anything. First, we did all the stuff we were supposed to do, like rinsing chlorine out of our hair and rinsing chlorine and crumbs out of our suits and wringing out our suits, and after we were done and all dry and we had put on a little of the white cream, like we were supposed to do when we got chapped and red on the lips between our legs, then we tried listening.

It was quiet out there. That was for sure.

Our scout came back with a full report. He had stopped flicking matches. Now Daddy was holding them between his fingers, letting them burn until they burned out.

Into our quiet, we heard him say, "Hey, girls, what are you, all dead in there or what?"

G o o d d a y, bad day, there were always lessons before bed. After us girls got ourselves ready—most nights wearing one of our daddy's big T-shirts, which even after a few nights still had the smell of our daddy on it, or some nights wearing a dry swimsuit to bed so that we did not have to lose time changing clothes in the morning—then our daddy stood up from his bed and started, he said, helping us to get smart. Up and back, down and front Daddy walked, stepping over wet towels and stopping to say, "Do you girls understand what I am saying?" and us girls saying, "Yes, Daddy," and "Is that the bear or is that the bull?" and our daddy slapping down a towel, saying, "Girls, girls, am I talking about this just to hear myself talk?"

That night, mostly, it was, as far as us girls could make out, about making losses into capital gains. There was also talk about the three *P*'s—pride, patience, and presentation—the last of which our daddy said mattered more than anything else, even for, and maybe especially for, a fellow in our daddy's own particular line of work.

"For instance," our daddy asked, "is it the *lady* or the *missus* of the house? And would you say say *rep* or *representative?*" our daddy asked, waiting to go on until one of us offered *rep* and another of us tried *representative,* and our daddy said that hearing it now he was pretty sure that *regional manager* was what would, after all, hands down, get a foot in the door.

"Mostly," our daddy said, turning back to folding and stacking towels, "men don't even think about these things. But girls, think about it. Please, girls, for goodness' sake, just try and think."

If we girls were thinking at all by that hour, and by that hour there was only one of us, at best, left enough awake to have half a thought and to watch through spidery lids our daddy cross and recross the hotel floor, stopping to make sure the DO NOT DISTURB sign was hung on the door and setting the flimsy door chain and crossing the room to the bathroom, where our daddy would get out his kit to give himself, he said, his well-earned lather and shave, all of which, especially the slap of minty aftershave, according to our daddy, mattered; and this was, by the way, exactly what he had meant, he said—if us girls were buck enough to still be up getting smart—what he had meant by the unseen details that make up Presentation—capital *P*.

NEXT HOTEL after the hotel after O'Farrell, our daddy announced that he was Mr. Homer, with a business specializing in exploration. For us girls the change to Homer meant nothing, just a little longer in the pool rechoreographing our synchronized water ballet so that we were no longer the Somersaulting Shamrocks, but now, with an extra dolphin and two tucks, we were the Sirens, which we decided was, of course, a better routine altogether, in the end.

"Excuse me, but would this be the head of household?" we heard our daddy ask. He talked oil and assets, cash flow, and mining, and we could see that Mr. Homer was moving now, the way our daddy discussed operations offshore and calmed the ladies about the particular ventures and discussed drilling and the modernization of refineries, all with a joint concern for improving quality and increasing dividends.

We knew business was good by the stacks of quarters our daddy left out for us so that we could get our soft drinks and our crackers. There were always quarters left for our lunch, which was a bar of chocolate split into just enough pieces for us girls to make sure we had a portion from each of the basic food groups.

There were families at this pool. There were mothers in two-piece suits, straddling chairs, spreading lotion and herding children under umbrellas when the sun was straight up and doing its worst damage. The fathers were out, too, racing their children freestyle. Us girls could see the fathers were cheating, not really even trying, and just letting the children go ahead and win. There were boards and rafts and blow-up floats. There was some kid's father on a bobbing alligator, saying, "Well, isn't this the life!"

It was best for us with the kids after lunch. Those kids were not even allowed to dangle feet, waiting out their half-hour digestions, and us girls, seeing them for the audience they were meant to be, took our places and did the Sirens and then—because we could—we did it again the old way as the Shamrocks with the extra front somersault.

It was the mothers whispering, the fathers coming up behind to hug kids that told us girls we had them, that we could do the triple dip for an encore, that no one was saying boo, that us girls had them—father, mother, kid—deflated creatures every one.

MR. HOMER was shouting.

Yield.

Liquidity.

Net.

We could see things through the drapery—shoes, maps, a lamp, our father standing on the bed.

He was jumping. He was dropping to his knees.

We could see the phone.

We could see they heard him, too, the mothers leaning in to catch a peek, a father floating over to ask, "Exactly what is your father's line of work?"

But down to the pointed toes, we were Daddy's girls—fast learners, backstroking out in star patterns, pike-diving under and coming up ready for the next move—a dip, a swerve—no nose-clipped, earplugged, afraid-of-the-deep kids were we. We were girls who sculled right past other fathers, saying, "Profit, profit, profit."

Our daddy, we could see him pacing between beds.

Volume.

Growth.

Market share.

We were sharks, cutting close to walls, angling underneath the shut-eyed floaters.

UP FRONT.

No credit.

A dollar bought fifteen minutes.

It was best taught in groups, we said. Sisters, brothers—we took any kid who could pay. It was waiting list only late in the day when the fathers, sunburned, were ready to nap and thought a couple of dollars a cheap way to steal an hour.

We kept those kids in the shallow end.

They wanted dives and fancy turns.

We said remember the *P*'s—posture, position, and practice. A ten-class ticket bought results. The bunny breaststroke, the tuck were things—if these pipsqueaks could only listen—that we would be getting to tomorrow. Sometimes we made them pay just to watch us. There was a lesson and a half, we said, in learning to watch. And did they know what to even look for, did they have the slightest bit of a clue of what they'd been looking at all afternoon, we asked. Well, by now they better, we said, or were we talking just to hear ourselves talk?

We held class until the fathers woke, chilled and pulling towels over themselves, and the mothers folded the sun reflectors and gathered up flip-flops and terry robes and books and called out to their kids, who we half-expected would also be picked up and stuffed right down into their mothers' giant bags.

It was then we looked up and saw our daddy. He was at the sliding window, the orange curtains draped around him. He was so bright, our daddy was, caught in the last angle of afternoon light, burning. He waved. His eyes were opened wide against the sunlight.

We held up to him the bathing caps filled with dollars.

"Come, girls," our daddy called.

"This family is going places," he said.

The curtains moved, undraping Daddy, and it looked to us like our daddy was at the very least a god taking the day back into himself, himself, the flaming end.

A wind stirred, dollars lifted, fluttered, a few landing on the pool. We did not dive for them.

"You see?" our daddy said. "So smart. My girls."

MOTHERLAND

nother time, my father says he has crossed mountains. He tells me he was less a boy than a shaggy goat scabbling a scree field, carrying his father and his mother and his mother's suitcase of photographs. Up there, somewhere where my father says you take two breaths for every step, his father's ring of factory keys was just noisy music. "There were fish in the rock," my father says. "But who was fishing?"

Now my father turns the boy south. This is later or earlier, or just another time when my father is a boy, a boy, he says, who tells his mother to leave her suitcase of photographs by the side of the road. "Then you will have to leave me by the side of the road," my father says his mother said. "But I was already finned and gilled," my father says. "A boy ready to swim seas."

"But, of course," my father says, "of course there were mountains under the water."

MY FATHER says, "I sold the ring of factory keys to a woman with no hands. I would have sold my father, too," my father says, "but the woman said she had no use for a father." Then my father says, "Bedrock." My father makes a fist, then shakes his fingers in the air. "Do you see what I am saying?" my father says. "Up and under," my father says, "the mountain ridges were a busted zipper, broken teeth of nickel and iron."

My father says each night he lifted the lid of his mother's suitcase of photographs and took a photograph to cover his face while he slept. My father says, "Bickering, goading, the dreams I had were not my own. The mountains moved," my father says. "First they shook, then they folded. The crust slipped, but I had already slit the hems of my father's and my mother's coin-heavy coats and I bore them up, two fringed black wings flapping off of my shoulders."

"I should have known, of course," my father says, "that from the air the mountains were great waves breaking."

MY FATHER says the next time he saw the ring of factory keys, it was hooked on the crooked nose of a man with no arms. My father says he bought it back from the man with no arms, who peddled the ring of keys as sacred music that opened the gates to a temple where God knelt to pray. "Because," my father says, "hem-slit and coinless, my mother needed weight to hold her to the road."

"On the road, there were no soldiers," my father says, "just Sons of Mothers caprioling in formation."

My father says that when the dry winds ruffed through the stunted timber, he licked tears from the faces in his mother's suitcase of photographs. My father says, "Broken heart, thwarted hope, the sadness I felt was not my own." By the time the Sons of Mothers finished their leaping march, my father says that he was all length and girth, reptilian, a boy down in the grass, snaking through lines of national boots, sleeping curled in the masonry of abandoned buildings. "Limbless, lidless, long belly to the rock," my father says, "I could feel the abrasive cut of running water gullying, dragging, gouging valleys out of mountains."

Then my father says, "Watershed."

"NOW WE are not alone," my father says.

"My father," my father says, "said he wanted to go home. I stood him at the foot of his shadow and said, 'Here is the threshold; step in.' "

This is another time, sometime after the ring of factory keys has been sold and bought and sold again to the head of a bodiless woman propped in the elbow of a tree. "Before I left," my father says, "I stole the ring of keys back from her—because I could."

Growling, gnashing, by the time the Other Mothers' Sons broke formation and charged, my father says that he had taken a photograph from his mother's suitcase of photographs and laid out for them a guest's and a groom's portion from the wedding feast. "They ate. They belched," my father says. "And when they slept, they were little babies sprawled and sucking at my mother's chest. Above tree line, there were plants in the rock," my father says. "But who was harvesting?"

The boy my father says he was has turned north. Melted ice. Crushed rock. My father says that when he was thirsty, he opened his mouth and drank the glacial milk. Sheets of ice drifted, sliced, piled. My father says, "But I was already cold-blooded and tailed, gripping the bank of a basin lake, my sticky amphibian tongue rolled out to catch what came my way."

"Of course," my father says, "of course I should have known that a running stream will grind out a plunge pool."

"OF COURSE," my father says, "cold rain fell."

The banks overflowed, the rift valley filled, but my father says he climbed into his mother's suitcase of photographs and ran the bulging rapids to where they eddied out. In the distance, there were cairns, my father said, but when he came close upon them, he saw they were just his mother's and his father's coins rolled downhill and piled in banker's stacks.

"What were hailstones," my father says, "but just pearl onions of layered ice?"

My father says the port was west, so he went east.

"When my father," my father says, "said, 'I am lost,' I told him to shake his ring of factory keys so that he would always hear where he was going." My father says the Horsemen mounted from the leeward slopes, but he was already a botfly, larval and boring down to what blood could be sucked. Rearing, bucking, tail-swiping, the agitated horses carried my father, he says, while he slept spun in a pupate sleep, his fibrous shell thorned deep in them.

"Under the noon sun, the coins melted," my father says. "And I gave my mother and my father the rightful bath of a queen and a king."

Then my father says, "Magma."

WHEN, finally, the Other Mothers' Sons lifted my father's mother and waved her, a glorious red banner of the motherland, from their bayonets, "There was still," my father says, "blood pumping through all four chambers of my heart. My father," my father says, "was the vest I wore when shots were fired and the lightness I felt was the lightness of human legs, mine alone, still running."

My father says that he opened his mother's suitcase of photographs on the other side of the mountain, but there were no faces left in the photographs. "Air-filled hat, empty shoes," my father says. "The aunts and the uncles I spoke to were not there."

My father says that somewhere he saw waves reaching shallow water, swinging parallel to the shoreline and hitting the shore head-on.

"When I arrived at the gate with my father's ring of factory keys, there were others with rings of keys already ahead of me on line. I saw God doubled over inside," my father says.

My father says the bending of a wave is called refraction; and then, though this is earlier, my father says, "Latitude."

At the other end of the line, my father says, there was another God. "Like this," my father says. "The Other God lifted his hand and in one motion drew the twist of goat, the wind of snake, the updraft of bird." Then the Other God's hand drew the thrust of the mountain, and then my father watched the Other God watch gravity take the mountain down.

"I am not horned or scaled," my father says.

"I am not a boy," my father says.

"Tell them," my father says, "that I am just a breasted man who dozes in an easy chair. And tell them that I am not a man who looks like—even if he had to—he could manage to carry even his own mortal form."

IN THE NORTH HOUSE

We see boats. Upriver from your city is where we live. Sometimes tugs. Sometimes barges loaded full. Sometimes storybook boats hauling their slabs. We know what we are looking for—men on the boats wearing high rubber boots. Our mother wears high-heeled shoes even in winter. Our mother in the kitchen makes tight turns between the stove and sink. Where she goes, go we, Hula Hoops around our waists. At night we hear her, the click and thuck and clap of heeled slippers on the stairs. Mother says yours is a city of all the hours, that after cargo is unloaded, men walk out into a midnight bright with people and light, where, smelling of diesel and fish, they can peel down their high rubber boots and find a hall where they might dance. Mother says the waltz is a boatman's dance, it having the wave's dip and crest. When she finds us, she finds us feet and arms and woolly animals down among blankets, pillows bunched, and sheets wrapped for turbans around our heads. Constantinople. We are her Persia. Our night is the pucker and suck of wind through plastic sheeting on windows.

Come morning, braids tucked up in shipmen's caps, we spot for morning boats. We see boats but not a single boatman, not boot, not cap, but the boastful flap of company flags. There are ospreys. We are ready to walk out over the quick-breaking ice to bring he who tumbles overboard from his sleep hammock in to where Mother stirs our cereal. He is not there. The ice thins and groans. The osprey hovers, plunges, breaks water feetfirst. Our mother calls us down. Calls us her handsome cabin boys. We are girls.

Is it true that you have ballrooms where women can go to dance alone?

By noon we are elbow-deep in red dye, dyeing satin from a dead woman's curtains. There will be dresses and vests and even, Mother says, yardage to raise our own wanton flag. Mother cannot keep a Hula Hoop up, though she says she has hips enough to balance her litter of young. Mother's house is vase and pillow, sofa and pot, this and that she buys at other women's houses. Shoes. Shoes. Stockings. Hair things. Soon even the washed-thin bedsheets have been dunked. You know what they say, says Mother, how a boatman builds a widow's walk in every port. I guess I think you see silk and satin on every corner, stepping up into buses, going down into trains. Women. Our stained arms, Mother says, are opera gloves. "Go blond," Mother says, "go black, it hardly matters. Yours truly named you," Mother says, "and that's what counts."

What counts for us is Mother's satin, dyed red in a kitchen sink. And arms, hers, ours, stained high and higher. What counts is the low grunt of breaking river ice and us running—double, double, double stairs up— to Mother's bed to sight a barge with letters we have never before seen painted on a gray side. What does not count is a woman dead in a house upriver or Mother saying, "Even the best of us gets picked over clean." What counts are boots, the thick rubber tread, the shank, the shaking off, a hallway corner piled knee-high with boots. We do not see a single boatman on the barge.

Soft in the middle, Mother's bed is a rolling-in place. We walk the edge. We walk the incline in. Haul on the bowline. Keep to the edge. Look out. We look out. The osprey is a dark angle over her feeding ground. When we come down, we come down one step at a time, heeled, hobbled in shoes too large, bulges from the funny press of someone else's foot, and ready to redden anything, everything that will take the dye.

Mother says that our boy-slim hips are blades that—watch out!—will one day kill a man.

Shaking, waggling, she cannot keep the bright hoop up. "Hell! Here is all my booty!" Mother says, and she is jigging toward us, leaving our Hula Hoops in the wake behind her.

Mother says in your city men dressed in tuxedos lie on the opera house floor so that they can hear the singing, but, "Please," Mother says, "they should never see the singers."

The ospreys who feed off our straight of river have nested in these cliffs for all the time I can remember.

At night, wool and limb, we are her Persia.

Do you still work the routes?

IT IS now the one long day of February that lasts all the month long. We wear hats. We wear scarves. Our opera gloves are covered over in striped mittens. Mother leads us, picking her way around the drifts that slope off from the window frames. Her heels drill into packed snow. We are her goslings, following, goose-hearted, looking south. Mother says there is one thing sweeter than a clothesline in July, and that, says Mother, is a line hung in the dead of winter. Now nothing, neither man nor fowl, darkening the river sees our satin curtain rigged, hung straight, thickened with water and cold. Mother does not wear a coat. Up here, where the river winds lift and circle, we make snowmen, armed, faces streaked red from where dye has bled down near Mother's feet. We have seen our ospreys perched together on the branches of the dead elm, but now there is only the chickadees' quick cross from the elm to the feeder, the scatter of seed, and Mother saying, "Will you look at this!"

Is it true that there are no mothers in your city but only women in furs going in through heavy doors?

We roll snow bodies uphill to where Mother takes her time—clipping, posing, hooking heels over the drying line—but when we get there, there is only a path of poked snow, and from somewhere Mother shouting, "Is this *red* or is this red?"

We leave our snowman, headless yet, to go to where we find her squatting at the seam of cliff trees. Mother lists to one side, hangs back from her underclothes, steam rising from where her current bores into snow. There is not a boatman in sight to raise a bottle for our fireship, or to the satin that Mother says is bound to blind and run a sailor into rocks. But Mother stays down, haunched, clitted, dress bunched in one hand and the round of ass a day moon risen. Soon enough, not even soon enough, these snowmen will be in the runoff south like all the rest.

We do not care if you cannot remember our names. Just call us all together, just take us with you to a dance hall and let us watch you do a waltz.

S U R E , okay, yes, we have killed. And not just our winter starved mice or summer's silly bunched slugs lunging the sweet, leafy air. There have been captains, shad fishers, sailors, clippermen, even the occasional barge cook up for a breather. Long before they knew what to know, long before they saw her, a bright red wave of skirt on the riverbank, they were spotted from this high place, high on the river cliff. Raised. Sighted. Pop-shot. If necessary—were you able to turn from the curve of her arm? If necessary, we will do so again.

It is a dangerous time.

We have killed, but we have never found body or bone of a single man. Bones, yes, there have been bones—mouse and cat, the rack and hip of deer we strap on as masks, or the rotted, soft spike of fish backs that Kitty carries triumphantly up to Mother's bed. We have found the twiggy bramble of abandoned cliff nest and the twiggy bramble of nest where our osprey lifts herself up from her new ones to come at us squalling her frenzied *cheereek, cheereek, cheereek.* We have found bottles, cans, combs, knotted ropes, boots, boot soles, knives, compasses, oars, and bullets hove upriver, we guess, off more than one slippery deck. But still we have found no men.

NIGHTS in Mother's bed, we wear the compasses strung around our necks, the little red North man in his North house, so that come morning we can chart the drift and current of our sleep. We fall asleep to the names of Mother's men—a sailor Bob and a Captain Jack—and wake to hear her, heels and spatula, downstairs. Come morning, wherever the North man has gone—around Cape Horn, through the Greenland

Straits—he is back, fixed in his North house as if we do not turn even once all night.

We have slept too well.

Captain Jack. Captain Kidd. You. She might have gone anywhere. . . .

Outside, the dead woman's curtains are sheathed in ice, a corner cut out, and we jump stairs—double, double down—to see, sure enough, Mother is red this morning, strapless and fitted, the satin a glazed ice over her hips.

And what a noise is this mother! Kettle and pan. Cleavage. The hum, the heels, the sizzle, the mutiny.

Breakfast is coddled eggs in cups, spinach nests, and soft cheese blankets that Mother says will put some meat on our bones. Breakfast is pancakes stacked and fruit unfrozen from summer's yield. There are muffins and biscuits, bacon strips and split sausage, the buckle of skillet ham.

She cannot stop cooking.

Mother says by spring one of us, braids pinned under a middy's cap, will be stowaway, our rosy, cabin-boy cheeks the treat of both captain and captain's wife. Each of us swears she is not going. Slim-hipped boys, we are her girls.

The morning boats are passing, sounding salutes for the brightly dyed banner of the dead woman's satin. Is it true that the children in your city are alley cats, going down to the docks to feed on spoiled goods? Mother is handing us plates, bone china brought home, she says, from another empty Nancy's house. She is mincing, she is whipping, she is chopping, is grating, is beating. There are soups and casseroles ready for freezing, sandwiches with crusts cut off, cookies in the shape of stars, of ships, a chain of girls in high boots. Roasts, chops, there are patties shaped by Mother, who does not turn from her stove to see if what passes is barge or raft or tug.

We practice knots—slip and bow, granny and clove.

Each of us swears she is already gone.

IT IS almost never now that we see our osprey out hawking over the shallows. Here, it is spring, muddy. We see boats plow past, churn up a river brown and thick. The osprey sits her nest. We have no time for Hula Hoops. We have read in a book on Mother's table that Constantinople is not called Constantinople anymore. We call our mother's bed Our Bed. The plastic sheeting is off the windows. We have read that there is a truer North outside the North man's house. At night from Our Bed, we can hear the midnight run to your city, the chatter of boatmen ready to step off of the river to dry land.

We say Mother is a red sail coming about in the mouth of your harbor. We say Mother is high boots and a jacket, another mate leaning against a column, watching a woman dance. She is a fur coat entering buildings. A tuxedo. Mother is the opera house floor.

If you see her, tell her there has been no flooding.

Tell her that we have scared off the women who have come looking for a good deal, for a this or a that, for something left behind. If you see her, tell her it is called Istanbul.

Tell her, please, do not come back.

BOXCAR

I t was not a place the boy could say he had come to before. They had been sitting in the car, how long? (the boy could not say)—with the father up there in the front seat, redded ears, shaved swatch at the back of his neck, the one hand the boy could see, with the knuckles pinned to the steering wheel. The father was up there (mutter, mutter, mutter)—and the boy thought it was no time to drive his red truck. But the red truck in the boy's hand kept moving, traversing the plastic seat, bumping down into the ditch between his legs, wedging in the wall of the boy's knees.

"And that's another thing, too," the boy heard the father say.

The boy looked up, over the back of the front seat, past where he could see his father, to the street, where the boy could see no one walking past. Nor could the boy say that he had never not come to that place before.

THEY WERE there, still parked, when lights came on and the boy saw men coming from all directions toward and by and always past their car. He saw a print of leaves stenciled on the car window. He saw past the window to where leaves had wadded, trampled wet and thick into tire ruts.

"It wouldn't kill you, really," the father said.

Under his shoes, the boy found pieces of leaves, muddy, mashed into the tread of his soles. He picked—pulled a stem out, whole. The boy let it drop onto the jackknifed truck, belly-up on the car seat. Out there was the woolly bulk of coats, men moving, a bright leaf hanging off a man's collar.

"What do you say?" the father said.

"ZOOM," said the boy.

IT WAS loud, the talking. Beyond the wall of the seat where his father was a shape of his father, the boy could not see the father's mouth moving. He could hear it. He could hear the father's tongue the way it moved lazily through the mouth, troughed, pushing spittle into corners.

A car passed and the passing lights chalked the father's hand on the wheel.

He heard the father say, "Sir."

"Yes, sir," he heard the father say.

The boy wanted the father to start driving. The boy thought of places they had been, other places where the father had said, "Lock the car," and the boy had stayed in the locked car, driving his red truck over seat ridges, over the dash, over maps spread on the seat, until the boy had given way to whistling, believing that the right pair of sounds would bring the father back knocking on the car window, the father's mouth mouthing, "Just hurry and open it."

"Is that you, boy?" he heard the father say.

H E W O K E to find his hands bedded in the press between his legs. (Cold.) It was too dark to see his breath. (Cold.) He could feel the freeze of hair pricking in his nose.

The father was up there—still talking.

It used to be that the boy rode in the front seat, slept down in the father's lap, down in a gray smell of plastic and gasoline and wool trousers. Sometimes, the father woke the boy for hot chocolate. They ate hot dogs any hour they could find them. The boy saw the father lean on counters. They slipped under pay stalls. Things were pocketed. There were cities at dawn and road stands with men his father called Jack. His father put two fingers to the windshield when the train cars passed. Hopper car. Boxcar. Coal. Coal. Tender. The father said maybe they should just go and jump aboard and be conductors.

THE BOY made the pull signal when the rigs passed, and the truckers gave a draw on their horns.

Madeline.

Sweet Baby.

Iowa Lady.

The rigs had names.

The father said that maps were hooey, and the boy threw them out at the next filling station.

Madeline was a lady's name, and the father said that they had no truck with ladies.

Hopper was a freight car with big, hinged doors.

"Sir?" was what the boy heard the father saying up there.

THE BOY heard the sound of his father's boots crunching leaves. He knew sounds could sound bigger at night. Out there, his father sounded like something that was coming to get him. (Even his father's water on the pavement rose like something that might drown him.)

*　*　*

THE CAR was parked, and the boy could see that it was tomorrow, early, cars passing with lights still on.

The father was not in the car.

The boy locked the car locks, climbed over to the front seat, and whistled, but the whistling did not bring the father back to the car.

"Hooey, hooey, hooey, hooey, hooey," said the boy. "Yes, sir," said the boy. "It wouldn't kill you."

HERE WAS the father knocking, saying, "Open up," saying, "Get out," saying, "This Jack in the store knows about something he thinks I could get my hands on."

The father gave the boy a cup of something hot to drink.

"This is it," the father said.

The boy heard miles in his father's voice, two hundred by lunch, or maybe there would be no lunch at all. The boy could not guess. The boy heard the clatter of change, his father saying, "You got it, boss," and "Sir, I'm your man." And later, "Just who you talking to like that?"

The drink was too hot for the boy to drink.

The men in coats were back on the street, going somewhere, walking past them.

"Do I look how I feel?" asked the father.

The boy sipped from the drink.

"Just how *do* I look?" asked the father.

The father took the boy's drink, tossed it, the dark milk spreading in the air.

"All aboard!" said the father, and they were off, past towns and towns and once towns, past raked leaves, burning leaves, past awnings, past diners and quick stands where men tank coffee, talk news, and waiter boys lean on counters for years, reading comic books with heroes who shuttle out past stars, past planets, rocketing mapless, past Deneb, Polaris, skirting the Pleiades, spacemen out riding the dusty tails of comets, out and out and out, to a place where a boy, hearing no echo of a distant earth, could pilot himself to a glorious end.

CABLE WORK

*T*he name, I think, was Costiki, or maybe Costikian, or Costa, or something altogether plainer, a name such as Casi or Cost or, for that matter, Jones. But, really, the name hardly matters. Neither does the year, though of the year I am quite certain—because there was a song that I recall was being played over and over on our way to and on our way back from this Smith's house.

There was a low spanning bridge, I think, we crossed to get there. There must have been a chair, where I was folding—though I can hardly imagine that at that time I was folding anything—anyway, where I, or perhaps my mother, folded my clothes.

You must see by now that this might have happened to another girl, that I could, in some sense, tell all of this as if it had happened that way.

I recall that the mother helped the man.

House is a misleading word in this case, the site being a basement really, a sort of office or basement workroom in what, I suppose, must have been the man's house.

The man said, "Like this," and put the mother's hands into position on the girl. There was a cloth, a sort of gauzy undershirt, between the mother's hands and the girl's hips. The girl held a bar that was, I am almost certain, not so much above her head as somewhere just to the front of it. The walls were green. I suppose, again, that this is not entirely pertinent, but there comes to me now not only the green of walls but a greenness, a pallor, that was everywhere in that basement room. There was a green odor, too, of course—perhaps the smell of heated plastic or sticky cloth strips, or the sawed metal. Oh, but it might well have been the apple the man lifted from a table and bit into, this green odor, or greenish one.

The man said, "Keep out the sway."

The mother tilted the girl.

The girl was to keep her knees bent, almost hanging, as it were, between the held bar and her bent legs. I think I have only described the first time with this Costa man, though the girl and the mother went across the bridge several times. Other times, I suppose, fittings were involved—the bodice, for example, and later, at another time, the chin piece.

The mother asked the man many questions.

The house—the one with this basement office—was, I think, on a street with other houses.

The girl heard shufflings upstairs.

"You see that?" the man said. "You can see how far off she is," the man said.

There were molds and castings piled in corners of the room in what seemed no particular arrangement.

The green smell might just as well have been a kind of plaster smell.

The mother looked and said, "But, oh God, but that is really just a baby."

Though it seems entirely unlikely, the man must have been missing fingers—missing, that is, not all of his fingers, but parts of some of his fingers.

Because the mother said that she had heard somewhere that it was a way to ward off bad luck, the mother and the daughter got into the habit of holding their breath as they crossed the bridge. They could not always make it, snorting breath and laughter out in bursts.

The girl, I should perhaps say, was old enough to have breasts—or not breasts, exactly, so much as swellings.

The man inserted one of his partial fingers, the smoothed bulb, down into the plastic bodice. "This is a fit," the man said.

At some point, between the mother and the man, I seem to be certain, money was exchanged.

* * *

93

PLEASE DON'T make me sorry that I have mentioned breasts. The man was, in all respects, a perfect gentleman. Really, he behaved as any machinist or craftsman would—in love, I suppose, first with the making, the articulation of the parts, the rivets, the straps, the molded plastic, and then with the perfect functioning of the parts together, as if not simply, for example, an engine had been made to turn over but a whole car had moved, had eased out of a driveway, had turned down a street, and soon enough had swerved off a highway ramp.

Forgive me, I have pressed beyond my recall and am careening now toward or away from what?

I believe the last time I saw this Costick man was a day before or a day after a birthday. Mother was full of lift and celebration. I was wearing it by this point, sitting as you see I still sit, overly elongated, rigid. But then I was held so that my head, to focus on only one section, was held, or really made to rest, between the chin piece and the neck prongs. Forgive me, I know it is hard to picture this, and in truth, it does not matter, does it?

We drove through a town. I suppose, for that matter, that it was the very town where this Costikiyan's house was situated, my mother in search, she said, of a treat. Though, as I have said, it was sometime in the vicinity of my birthday, there was ice on the road, or at least something that made my mother lose the wheel for an instant, or at least just long enough for the car to start to spin. Held in place by the man's handiwork, I felt as if the car was turning around me but that I did not turn. I reached to hold on to something, to steady myself, I suppose, and probably grabbed the forward horizontal of the apparatus itself, gripping, as it were, my own corrected form. By the way, I think I could feel on the inner side of the horizontal some nicks cut into the metal as if a stylus had marked the spot in what, I guess I could say, was a designation, a signature of sorts.

The car came to its stop in exactly the direction and lane we were in at the spin's start. That song, the song I believe I have already noted, was, I believe, just ending or, maybe, just coming on the radio. Mother rolled open her window. We drove back over the bridge, Mother making it, she later said, in one breath. The bridge was a suspension bridge, tall towers rising from it at regular intervals. There were men connected by hook and belt to the cables. There was, I believe it was there, a rough grinding noise and the cold smell of cut steel.

The man, I remember, said, "This should do the trick."

Somewhere past the tollbooth, Mother said not on your life could anyone ever get her to hang from anything as crazy as that.

The realignment was, I understood, already in motion.

SOUL TO TAKE

I lay myself down in the middle, in the crack made by their pushed-together beds. Or I am not in the crack between their beds, but I am in one of their beds and he is saying, she is saying, "Come under my covers." An arm, his, sent out, tucks down, around, under me. She wears a sleep mask, crooked by now, the string cutting over, across, into a cheek. One of them swoodles my hair, gets a piece of it slipping around over her, his finger. Both of their arms are soft; one of their arms is hairless. This is Saturday. It is Sunday, and I am five, am nine, am thirteen. I am seventeen years old.

OR SOMETIMES their door is locked.

* * *

LIKE THIS, they fall back to sleep.

Like this, between them, an arm over me, a leg against my leg, I do not sleep; or if I sleep, I sleep in their sleeping, watery chortle and dry cough, in here, where sleep is the clustering sounds in his throat and the pinked dark at the base of her neck, and the loamy rise out from down in their sheets when one of them turns and the bedding lifts.

And they are always turning.

And one of them, awake now, says, "I cannot sleep a wink."

Or this is my bed, sometime after one or the other or the both of them have come into my room, one of them saying, "Shove over," and all of us bending, squinching, rebending on and around so that we fit, all three of us, puzzled and overlapped, in my single bed, the both of them, short and long breath, sleeping now.

YES, I understand about their locked door.

SHH, I think I can hear them.

AN ARM, his, stretches over me, stretching to where she sleeps curled away from him, from me. Or she says,

"Honey," and we say, "Yes," we two, where there are two honeys apiece in these twinned beds.

He, she, they are great fans of pajamas. If you want, lift the bedding. Take a look. See the piping, the ruffle. Here are drawstrings. She wears a bed jacket, lace appliqué and inset. Always striped and always cotton—he likes his pressed and a new pair every night. I wear what they give me: cotton pants cut short, a silk nightie with a split seam.

"Baby," they say, and I am their baby.

I am all the years old that I will ever be old.

AFTER THE LOCKED DOOR comes the unlocked door. There they are, the great mound that is they, the blanket, a ground healed over them. They are there, spill and mound and archaeology. Under I dig to find a wedge that they have opened for me to lie down in.

I lay me down to find a gummy earplug, pressed flat under a pillow or split on the sheet. I find the girth of his smell, or the back of her legs where my knees trench. Crumbs in the bed. A frayed hem. And hairs, hers, his. His shut eyes. Or her saying, "There you are." Or, maybe, maybe most of all, the cool place in the crack that their heat has not touched.

A slap, hers. The hand, his. His eyes are closed, but he is not sleeping. Someone is tickling. Someone is saying, "I've got you." He is rolling over, pulling blankets;

she is rolling over, pulling blankets. They are calling each other Mother. They are calling each other Father. I am in the middle, between them. They are wasting me. I could be anywhere.

HERE—on this side of the screen and the glass, this side of the shade and the drape—is the world.

ALWAYS it is a birthday in their beds. They say my name and name me their victory, victorious over all things outside of this room and in this room. I am frosting and cake and all ten fingers, bewicked and bright for wishing. I am the extra one for good luck. The record shuts off on the bedside Victrola. Here, Wynken, Blynken, and Nod are we. I am Blynken, blinking in the not-quite dark where they wink and nod and rock to labored sleep.

I do not sleep.

AND SOMEONE is saying, "Wake up, sleepyhead."

OR I have seen them.

I have walked in the unlocked dark to the foot of their beds, the sheets pushed down and ribbony down by their feet. I have watched his feet: the spur of his heel poked up in the air and his toes climbing down hard against the mattress. I have seen her feet airborne, seen their twitch and their jerk. I have seen her feet scrape down his legs to where she hooks her feet around his, the sheets caught now and slipped down, around and over them. I have seen their toes, curled and rigid, pried apart and reinserted.

"Baby," he says.

She says, "Baby."

I have seen the clench.

I have stayed there, down there at the foot of their pushed-together beds and watched their feet, their legs, the turn, the slow or fast fit of their taking. I have seen him, her, reach out like a whelp searching out the long nipple. I have seen her, I have seen him, taken in, licked clean; and when they are done, I have watched them fall back from each other to sleep.

S H H , they are sleeping.

N O W I lay me down, to wake in the seam, in the crack, in the place they make for me between their beds. Now they come to me, my two babies now nestling down against my arms. "That is my hair," she says, her fingers down and shuffling in my hair. He says, "That lip has my name on it."

Like this, they take me to them.

* * *

She says, "Let's get a move on."

Drapes are being drawn. Shades rolled. They are running water. They call me Rip Van Winkle. She picks crust from my eyes.

They say, "Up, up, up." They say, "Hey, lazy-bones, open your eyes."

They say, "Tell us your dreams."

I am Blynken, sailing out alone in the wooden shoe, with the owl and the pussycat onshore, waving hand-kerchiefs. I am Blynken taking catnaps in the heel of a shoe.

I am so tired.

They are leaning over me, shaking, shaking, shaking me awake.

I am Victoria.

WOOL

*T*hat summer, he waited nights out on the porch, sometimes with the child. Most times, it was just himself, a leg hinged over an arm of the wicker rocker or his whole self down flat against the porch boards, knobby backbone cracking when he would finally lever himself up to go inside to wake the child when it was no longer night. For so much of the day, it was not night. The days were for fixing whatever he could find to fix—rotted-out stairs, jiggly boards, his own twisted backbone that he tried to straighten, dangling off the porch railing till the child counted up twice to twenty and back.

That summer, the nights were for wool, and they wore it, wool socks, wool shirts—the child, floppy and handless in one of his sweaters, bunched in wool blankets and still not warm. He gave the child drinks from his drinks. Their breathing, he told the child, was sheep crossing, and they watched car beams shear the coats off their flock. He hung a roped whistle around the child's neck. He sent the child in to bed, but the child wandered back out to the porch with mittens and a hat and the whistle cut from its rope. They counted cars.

Nights, waiting, he watched the garden grow or claimed to the child that he could see it growing in the dark, creep of melon vines, pole beans shimmying up poles, tomatoes fattening on their sticks. The peppers and eggplants, he claimed, had burst the garden fence and were off and rolling down to town. They counted stars. When finally the child finally fell asleep, he kept at it, holding off his count until the cars passed close to the porch, the headlights running over him before the car was gone.

Some nights there were no stars.

It was wool in the mornings, too, with the child pulling him down the newly planked stairs to look at the garden. There were creakings. The grass was wet. The garden was frilly with bugs and weedy in the beds, where he had not weeded. He had not weeded at all that summer and what grew grew shagged and scrawny. The eggplant plants eaten, leaf and stem. He boosted the child up onto his shoulders in time to see a car pass on the road.

* * *

Wool

THERE IS a garden. There is a road. He is on the
porch. There is a child with all of a child's unruly love
of order.

You might drive this road any night of your life
coming back from or going to a job in any of some of
the towns where this road leads. There are curves.
There is the low place where the river floods in spring.
You know the houses stitched along the road and you
have seen in yards the strung-up lines of clothes. There
are bicycles, a dog snapping at the length of his chain,
the border ribbon of flowers. All the declarations of we
are here, we are here. You have seen the porch. Maybe,
yes, even certainly, you have seen them or some shape
of them at night, a movement, a rocking shape up here
that summer on this porch.

Up here on this porch, it was night, and when it
was morning, he was still waiting, the child waking fitted to him or coming to him tangled and cotton-eyed.

By midmorning, there were sweaters tossed on the
railing, pants rolled up, damp at the ankles, a dropped-
over mitten inside out and soon to be lost. He worked.
There was always another rotted-out board. There was
nailing where the newly planked boards had come un-
nailed. The child was there on the porch or in the yard
where he could watch the child. While he worked, the
child counted up to twenty and back and up and back
and up, counting whatever—porch boards, cars, something the child glimpsed in the air—whatever—the
child trailing through the yard until—so suddenly!—he

could not hear the counting and called and called and called until the child ranged back into his sight.

The child came back naked when the child came back, or almost naked, wearing a badge of dirt, a scatter of clothes threaded behind in the rag grass. Shirtless and shoeless, he was mostly naked, too, by then, his pants cuffed to just below his knees. He told the child that the body was also a garden and, checking, moved his hands up the child for what bugs might have fixed on the child's stalky legs.

He lifted the child up onto the porch railing. The child balanced on a leg, saying, "Don't catch me," until the child jumped and he caught the child and they both tumbled down. Down in the rag grass they were all skin. They were wet with his work sweat. They were knuckled and ribbed. Horsie, horsie, they rode a crooked back to town. They were straddled, mounted, crying uncle. They were kissing. They napped in the grass below the porch that summer, high noon passing over them, crisping their skin. They stood up, marked and scarred with grasses, weeds sprouting from the backs of arms, of legs. They stood up, holding nails and wood chips, and once a wool mitten was found in the grass before it was lost again. They were burnt-nosed.

A car passed.

For what were they standing there bare-chested in the overgrown grass, watching your car bounce down the road to town? For what was he waiting? Was that him in town—you think, Of course, it must be—a man alone or a man alone with a child wheeling in the fluorescent buzz of a market, stalled beside the case of frozen suppers, buying powdered milk? Was that him pulled off the road not far from one of the towns, the child on his lap gripping the wheel?

That summer, every meal was a picnic in the grass or standing in the kitchen, food in cartons, vegetables in cans, and a pudding they ate dry as a mix. They sprinkled salt into their hands. Pepper was for bread. He told the child that this was the way it had been for him as a child. He told the child there were gifts to send for, and forever that summer they were cutting box tops and licking stamps.

It was a summer of shooting stars.

It was a summer of flashing lights banding the Milky Way.

Each day the mail truck passed.

"They are coming," he said.

THEY DID NOT come in the high leaf of July.

What came in July was the down-road dog yanked free of its chain and tearing up the road. He sent the child inside. The dog came sideways up the porch stairs. He kept behind the wicker rocker. The dog snapped and lunged until he came out from behind the wicker rocker and beat it down with his hammer. His hammer came down on its back. His hammer came down on its head. He nailed its paws to the porch boards. The child stood in the doorway until he looked up and said, "Get some clothes on." When the child came back out—naked but for shoes—the dog was gone from off the porch. He was laying down new board. The child brought him one of his drinks. He tossed the drink, glass and all, into the rag grass. Birds came, circling over past the garden. The child napped in the wicker rocker through the long afternoon, getting up to pull on layers of wool until it was night.

Before it was night, it was evening. It was gold grass and a blue road down the hill to town. It was a fuss of birds back past the garden. It was someone down the road calling, "Here, boy."

There were nights without a moon and without stars when he and the child sat with their backs against the house and the rain slanted down on the porch. They wore ponchos. They folded themselves in under the ponchos and kept to the place on the porch where the rain could not get to. He listened to the stars or told the child he could hear them above the rain—the fizz of shooting stars, the groaning planets in their heavenly rotations. There were comets landing in the garden. There was thunder. Rain ran in rivulets down the grooved boards and he stacked loose nails to build a dam. He bet the child a bicycle that the rain would stop before the thunder stopped. They kept to their dry place on the porch until their dry place was too narrow to hold them side by side. He pulled the child onto his lap, their ponchos scratching out a vinyl rhythm.

It was not a night to turn your head from the road, to look to see them twirling under the porch light, or riding their ponchos down the muddy hill. It was a night for testing brakes, for windshield wipers, for defrosters on high, for holding anything you could find to hold—a newspaper, a paper bag—anything for lifting over a head and running headlong into doorways.

It was a night for calling in sick, for staying home.

IN THE MORNING, he stood on the porch, holding a bicycle above his head. The bicycle was green and rusty, grass laced in the spokes, a broken bell twisted on the handlebars, nothing that steel wool and a coat of red paint, he said, could not fix for new.

He held the bicycle up while the child climbed up onto the seat. The child asked where the bicycle had come from, and he asked the child if it was best that he should just go right now and bring the bicycle back.

"Don't let go!" the child said, and he let the child go, the child staying up for a count of four before tipping over.

He dragged the bicycle up to the porch and began to fix it. He scraped it down. He sanded it. He untwisted the twisted bell. When a car drove past, the bicycle was polished red.

He found the child, when he went to find the child, on the other side of the garden fence. The child was crawling through the weeds. There were rocks piled along a measure of fence. He told the child to come and the child slithered over to him. He lifted the child over his head and then lowered the child headfirst down into his lap. They were snakes in the garden, lying on heated rocks. They tested rocks with their tongues. When all of the rocks were too hot, they slid uphill, and by noon the child was riding red tracks through the grass.

A car drove slowly past.

WHAT DO YOU make of them, of him prying the porch stairs apart in August, board by board yanked and thrown into a heap, or of the child on a red bicycle that by August is beginning to show through patches of green? What do you make of the child, naked or bundled, a matted lamb of a child, frozen on the porch railing when you drive past and likely to be there still, now turbaned and fleecy in towels, when you come from town, taking the curves too quickly, passing over the dry riverbed that floods the road in spring, passing the checkered laundry lines, passing the child, who lifts a hand—to wave you on or down, can you be sure? And him, too, looking up as you pass as if to make sure that you are passing?

They are there in town, overdressed, running in the lot behind the county office or stopped on a road, cutting flowers from border beds.

A car drove slowly past.

"That's ten," said the child. The child was on the porch and he was down below, reframing, nailing in temporary struts.

"Everything's ten," he said, looking from the child, to the house, to the road, and back to the child. He held

up his hands and the child hitched over the railing, trying to snatch finger after finger.

There were cut two-by-fours leaning.

The car backed up to a stop in front of the house.
The car windows were rolled partway down.

"Hey, mister," someone called from the car.

He hoisted a two-by-four over his head. He jim-
mied the two-by-four into place.

"Mister, hey, mister," someone called.

He pulled nails from his pocket and stuck them between his teeth. He drove nails into boards until his
mouth was empty.

The car gunned its engine and pulled off down the
road.

"That's it," he said.

THAT WAS IT for August, before the ground frost
and after the showing of northern lights. The northern
lights wheeled neon above the porch, where they lay till
the night when the child sat up, saying, "I'm dizzy."

He walked the child around the house. The porch
wrapped now around the whole of the house, splitting
only for stairs and a ramp they walked down single file
to the garden, where the rocks looked ripe and ready to
be picked. The rocks were cool in their hands. Their
shirts were baskets they loaded with rocks and dragged
up the ramp of the wraparound porch. They settled the
rocks in a ring and set a fire with scrap wood they
pulled from under the porch. Hats, sweaters, they

sheared themselves down to their skins. Their skins were yellow near the fire. He showed the child how he could jump through fire and the child jumped after him, the flame licking the soles of the child's feet. The child's feet blistered and he put the child's feet into his mouth. The child's body was shivery with heat. He held himself over the child, giving the child his hand to bite. The child sucked and bit until there was a taste of blood.

IN THE MORNING, there was frost in the garden and the rag grass glittered like a heaven on earth. There was a hole burned through the porch boards and smoke drifted and hung over the sleeping bodies.

The child woke.

There was so much left to be fixed before winter.

RUBY, DARWIN, EURYDICE

*A*pril again, and this means little Holland.

She did it on her own, planting and planting. When? We never saw her planting, and then comes April, her only two months under and the tulips up. We never guessed there were so many kinds, so many colors; and more than just colors, there were colors off of colors, and edges, scalloped, pronged, squared, wisped, roughed, shredded, smoothed.

Are you looking? Are you standing at the porch window with our father in his business suit? Then you see his eyes scan the lawn as if he thinks he will find her down in a flower bed or high in a waxy cup.

WE COULD NOT get rid of enough tulips to keep our father from the window.

Every day, we went out with scissors, but the tulips were not like dandelions or other weeds; they were like the very blades of grass. By the armful and then by the cartful, we carried tulips to the woods behind our house. We threw, we dumped, and then, because we were afraid Father would see the mound of their bright heads, we got our mother's spade to dig a place to drop the tulips in.

We could not keep up with her tulips.

There were early plantings and then later ones that erupted glossy and striped. And Father, at the porch window, called the patchwork that glowed in the early light a miracle, a miracle that she had sent.

We brought our father a bulb so that he could see that the tulips were not a miracle but born out of the scaled potatolike bodies that she had stuck one by one under the ground.

Our father came home with tulips wrapped in florist paper to put in vases and then in bell jars about his bedroom. He said he wanted to sleep in a room with tulips covering every inch of room, but he could not stand to think of cutting a single stalk from her lawn.

When he was not looking, we cut some more.

Are you still with our father? Do you see then, even after the light has gone and there is only the dark-shadowed darkness, that he is still standing?

In the morning, we saw that Father's bed was still made as we had made it, the sheets pulled taut to keep our father safely in.

B Y M I D - A P R I L , Father started pointing. "Here is a Chellaston Beauty; those are Magnificents; here is a Ruby; those are Queen of Sheba," our father said.

When Father went off to work, we went into our mother's closet, took a few dresses, and then let the men load the rest into the charity truck.

T H E N E X T A P R I L , our father turned from the window.

We looked out to the overblown tulips, the last of their petals ready to unhinge.

When we turned back to Father, he was walking out the door in a seersucker suit.

A P R I L A G A I N , and this means little Holland.

We are down among the beds. There is always work to be done—cutting down finished blooms, keeping the weeds from choking back a single stalk; in November, there is planting the new varieties, the hybrids we have ordered from overseas. We work at night because we now believe that this is what she did, lifting herself from the side of our father and walking out across the black grass. By morning, we are back inside, calling our father to the porch window to see the miracle that she has sent. Father heads out the door, his arm trailing a cheerful wave.

"Look," we call after him, "there is Candy Stick, Parrot, Bijou, Golden Harvest, Golden Age, Darwin, Eurydice, Plaisir, Double Early, Double Late."

From out the porch window, we watch the April sky ball up dark, then open.

Do you see our father bent and running?

He does not see that with each of his steps—not once does he look back—our lawn begins to fade.

CHINA

*E*very day the sky was blue.

Every day the sky was blue.

Bone blue, the sky was, a color to wish the world could fall up into, a blue that made us thirsty. Aunt kept water jars lidded tight in cupboards, and still the flies found their way in. Spade said swallowing flies would make him strong. It was brittle grass where we stalked the field. Spore and seed powdered our lips. I was Spade's eyes, to show him where to step. Our prey was anything that moved—leaf beetle, peeper, walkingstick, katydid—I never caught any. Spade, he did, the katys and the peepers. And what it was to watch him, blind hunter, swipe an arm to snag a bug to pocket to go to school with, was not so great as how I got to school, to find my empty pocket gifted to the top with the smooth shells of his beetles.

That spring, nothing could be quiet. What was underfoot was loud—pop and break and break and mud dried shaley where there should be water. The brook was a twist gone rocky. Spade slipped to belly, ear to the ground, said he could hear water. I called him the Water King, held his hand to show him where to poke. He said, "No, Ellie, that's not where I hear it." Rock and rock, a toe to break loose rock gravelly, a cautious sister heeled to hold a slanting king, a brother, grave, saying, "I'll find it for her"—like that we wound our way up the brook bed.

All the rutty way home from school, I kept my eyes squeezed shut. The bus took the road past Aunt's house. But I could not make it, not the whole way, without unsqueezing my eyes to a flickery squint, and still, it was always Spade to say, "Ellie, this is home."

THE STORY on the bus that spring was the story of the watchman's lantern.

WE WALKED in the field in the morning toward what my brother heard. Where Spade could hear water, I heard the crackle of stalks, the kestrel's sharp *kle, kle, kle*. There was a place in the field where the grasses made a tent above Spade's head. It was here he said to dig. And dig, my brother did. By stick, by hand, he broke that field, pitting it to pull forth the fisted rocks.

I called my brother Spade for the digger that he was.

In the rocks, I found the trace of other things—a stem, a spiral, a moon-shaped shape, the backbone of a fish.

Spade said he smelled it, too, the rusty bite of water close to Aunt's house.

Spade called Aunt, Mother.

Spade was a thin-wristed boy, a flame of red hair for good ladies to make a mess of. Spade was a boy with eyes rolled way back, a boy to put a powdered cloth to Aunt's hands each night. Spade was small steps to my bed, him saying, "Ellie, it takes too long."

Nights on our knees, that was the spring they told us we needed to pray for rain. Long after I had asked for what I needed, a length of blue ribbon, a suitcase, a voice I would remember, there was Spade in his dark, praying, "Rain, rain, rain."

I called Aunt, Aunt.

THE STORY went that the watchman's lantern would not light.

THE FIELD began to look like the field in fall.

The hatch had mostly died.

The clouds that came to graze above the field were clouds that Aunt said meant nothing about nothing. There was not a single wisp, not a whisper of something blown off the bottom or the top of any bulging cloud, not a cloud among them to gather to any promise.

Spade kept digging.

Spade kept digging.

The kestrel turned red-backed above the field.

The clouds wandered out of our field's view.

Where the field led to the brook at one side, at the other side it led to the forest. The witch hazel edged in understory along the incline up through sycamore. There it was still green, but Spade would not go, declaring that the water was close to Aunt's house.

When Spade said, "Ellie, do you hear it?" what I heard was the sound of Spade digging.

Good ladies came to Aunt's house. I brought Spade in from the field for them to press lemon drops into his hand. When there were ladies, there were bottles of soda and there was Aunt's raisin cake served on plates we dry-wiped clean after the ladies had talked their talk of wells and stood to run their crumbed hands through Spade's hair. The pipes ran knock and suck, barely spit to wash a glass. The ladies smoked cigarettes. They talked and their cigarettes burned to ash in Aunt's saucer plates. When they were gone, Spade carried the empty soda bottles out to the brook to set for ants. The ants, they always came. The flies came, too. They worked the empty bottles, working down into the clear barrel. Crowding for what? I could not see.

* * *

THE STORY of the watchman's lantern, we had
heard before—the watchman in the dark trying to light
his lamp.

SLOW WAS how fast Spade was with her. Aunt's
hands were nothing I would have touched. But touch
Spade did and more, working the cloth down into the
web of her fingers, ringing the open blisters, powder-
ing even where the bitten skin fringed her cuticles.
Aunt closed her eyes. The lids over her eyes were
blue. Outside of Aunt's house, it was dark. Here was
in the house and out there was the field and here
there was the window where the beetles fixed on the
glass and the moths tapped their wings. The light
shone through their wings. Their wings were white
and their wings were green and a lacewing had wings
that threw a shadow on Aunt's floor. There were
things that came to the window whose name I did not
know. I told Spade what I saw. I saw the billbug and
the luna moth. I saw Spade hold Aunt's hands one
hand at a time. I saw a cradle moon tipped above the
field.

I saw this, and there was more.

I could not tell Spade everything that I could see.

MATCHES, rags, gasoline, an automobile ablaze,
and still the watchman's lantern would not light.

* * *

THERE WERE things I would touch.

I would touch the spiraled rocks we brought in from the field, the moon-shaped shape, the slick of Spade's hair when he came, dream-tossed, to my bed, saying, "Ellie, I am too tired." There was Spade's hair, the crossed veins of his thin wrists to touch, and I would touch the milky place of Spade's rolled-back eyes even after Aunt said, "Just stop it now!" Surely, I would have touched the lacewing's coppery eyes, but I was not as fast to the window as Spade was fast to snap a fly that buzzed near Aunt's feet. Not her hands and not her feet and not the worn linen of Aunt's dress, not any of this of Aunt and more of Aunt would I have touched even for a length of blue ribbon, even for a woman's voice I could remember.

The moon-shaped shape was not exactly the shape of any moon there was that spring.

MATCHES, rags, gasoline, an automobile, a stand of trees, a house, two houses, the county school, neighboring fields, neighboring towns, all the neighbors' neighbors, and still the watchman's lantern would not light.

NOTHING GREW.

Then nothing grew.

Then the sky was brown with the hang of a duster and dust came in through the cracks and dust came in through the sashes and when the dust settled, the bill-bugs and the luna moths and the katydids and the walkingsticks were all in a powdery sweep on Aunt's floor.

More came in. And more.

Spade said that he felt strong from swallowing dusty bugs and he was on his way to dig through not to a spring or to a brook but to a great wide ocean. I watched Spade make his way out through the field. I watched Spade trip on the pitted places of the holes he had dug, till Spade was on all fours in the field, feeling his way in the field to a place in the field for him to dig.

I followed.

The sky was brown. The leaves of the witch hazel and the leaves of the sycamore were brown. We crawled through the field. The dust was so thick inside of Spade's ears, he said he could not hear a drop of water. I told Spade I heard water. I told Spade I heard water and a woman's voice, and Aunt was our mother, and the ladies who came to tousle Spade's hair were each our good mother, and the kestrel was our mother, and the sky was black with the press of rain. I told Spade that at the one side of the field, the leaves of the sycamore and the leaves of the witch hazel were bent to rain. I touched the milky place of Spade's rolled-back eyes and said, "There. There. There," till Spade said, "But, Ellie, don't you see, the sky is blue."

* * *

THE STORY on the bus that spring was not the story of how the world burned.

I WOULD LIKE to say that by morning the rain had come. I would like to say that the rain had come and filled the dug holes in the field and that we stood in the field, Spade and I, and the rain came down without a letup for all the days and nights, and that school that spring was called off because of flooded roads and not because the school's well had run dry. I would like to say that when I touched the milky white of Spade's rolled-back eyes then Spade could see the field and the place beyond the field where the witch hazel and the sycamore greenly grew. I would like to say that I found the trace of a woman in a rock and that when I brought the rock woman into Aunt's house, she turned into our mother and took us from that house and from that field to a place where the june bug feasts on ripe peaches and the kestrel hovers for prey.

I will say instead that Spade was boy, a lemon drop of boy, a rakish spunk of a boy and I was Ellie, blind as a watchman who slept outside a burning town.

I will say rain came.

It is true what they say about thirst.

THE WATCHMAN was not a brave man. The watchman was not brave, nor was he clever, and when he sat down with his back against a stone wall, he quickly fell asleep. Thieves came and stole his shoes and his hat. When the watchman grew cold, he had a dream. In his dream, the watchman's wife came to him, looking as she looked when she was just a young girl. So delighted was the watchman that when he woke, he believed that his wife had truly come, unlaced his shoes, lifted his hat, and was girlishly hiding close by. When the thieves returned to steal his clothes, the watchman stepped willingly out of his clothes, believing that the thieves were friends his wife had brought along for the trick. The night was cold. The watchman began to shiver. So loud was the clacking of his teeth that the watchman did not hear the thieves returning a final time.

Spade said that he did not think that the thieves would return, since they had already stolen everything that they could from the watchman. Spade said, "Ellie, it was the wife that the watchman could not hear." Spade said, "The wife was out looking for the watchman." I did not say, "No." I did not tell Spade that the wife was back in town with the neighbors and the neighbors' neighbors—that the wife, like all the rest of them, was burning.

I WOULD NOT shovel the dirt back into the hole they dug for Spade.

In the house, the ladies nodded their heads. The ladies drank their sodas. Aunt rubbed her eyes. I was not there to see the sycamore limb split and fall.

"And now this," Aunt said.

I did not walk out in the field in the morning with Spade. I did not show him the way. I had told Spade I did not care anymore what the katydid did or what the katydid does or what the katydid will never do.

And still the sky was blue.

Where there had been the break and drop of limb, what had Spade heard?

If I were fast as Spade was fast, I would break the limbs from off the ladies.

The hole they dug for Spade was dug from a hole Spade had dug.

HE SAYS, "Mother, tell me a story from your mouth."

He calls me Mother. And I am.

There was a boy, I tell him, who dug and dug down, not to a spring but to a great wide ocean. The boy saw a man sleeping on the bank. The boy could see that the man was sleeping, although the man's eyes were wide open. The boy shook and shook the man until the man blinked and woke and waking cried, "Thief, thief, take my lantern. Here it is." In the boy's hands, the lantern door opened and out flew the luna moth and the walkingstick, and the moon-shaped shape and the school bus. The boy opened his mouth. Then from the blue sky, it began to rain.

AVENGE! AVENGE!

R ight off the bat, let me introduce Vinnie, Fred, Frank, Artie, Tony P., Tony D., and Tommy DeRay.

Fred and Tony D. work the phones, so when some asshole blasts in their ears, "Sell silver ten dec at a quarter," the boys pink-slip it and pass it on to Tony P., who gives it to the broker big shot in the ring. They pull in Frank and Vinnie when it gets heavy. That leaves Tommy DeRay to check trades with me, and Artie to do yesterday's sheets and work out the breaks.

But today, you could call it a slow day, so Tony D. and Fred have started calling numbers. They get themselves on the phones and dial to where a girl comes on, saying that, Baby, yes, she is so wet and that she's got herself half-jacked rubbing the phone over her amazing bongers, and Tony D. and Fred's job is to go ahead and repeat all what she says all out loud to all the rest of the guys.

Not to sound snot-ass or anything, but I am too busy for that slow-day bullshit. I write these stories. Mostly, I write these legends that take place in the far-distant historical long ago.

"Come on," Tommy DeRay says, "if you are looking for a good story, start with the story of me. Say Tom DeRay is a guy who lives off Utopia Parkway with his mother and his sister. Say Tom DeRay has a silver Trans Am that everyone in the neighborhood treats with the utmost respect in the hopes of them getting themselves a lucky ride."

"Great, great," Tony P. says, "just what we need, another story about a nobody pussy living with his mother in Queens."

Fred puts his hand over the mouthpiece on the phone and says, "Tell about how we worked our asses off the week silver was limit-up every day of the goddamn week."

"Great!" Tony P. says. "How it was limit-up and the brokers were wiping their sweet asses with bars of silver while we walked our skinny butts home with our same pissant paychecks. Hey, please. I'm looking for a story where a guy like me is the winner."

"Then tell the one," says Vinnie, "about the day when the world market came to a standstill because someone looked out the window near the crude ring and saw two people who'd gone up to the roof of the next building to lay a little lunchtime pipe, and before you can say 'Buy augie at ten,' everyone is jamming the window to watch these two cuties get cute. Every local and every two-dollar man is at the window fighting down a boner while this chick on the roof has got her skirt up over her head. Then tell how over there in Hong Kong whoever the fuck the fuckhead is who stays the fuck up to watch the New York board is saying, 'Velly stlange—velly, velly stlange.' "

"Man, if you had just let me finish, you would have heard something about a hard-luck guy who came out a winner," says Tommy DeRay. "You would have heard about how I come home one day to find that someone has taken a knife to the tires and to the paint work on the Trans Am. The car looks bad. It looks worse than bad. I go out of my mind nuts fucking crazy. I'm fucking standing in front of my car and I'm not fucking joking that I'm screaming, 'Avenge! Avenge!' "

"And then," Tony P. says, "then you burst out of your clothes and you're in the tights and cape of our favorite superhero, Queens Boy. Ta da! You look out and see across the great metropolis of Queens with your super vision to where some local no-goods have holed up in a pizza joint, eating slices and laughing at their latest caper."

"No man, all of you are dead wrong," Tony D. says. "What we really need is something really deep. Like how it felt the first time you smoked your first joint and thought about your life and the whole thing was one deep revelation, one completely revelating revelation."

"Oh Mama! Praise the Lord and spare us!" says Tony P.

"No man," Tony D. says. "I'm fucking serious. Top this, man. I'm fucking talking about bong hits in a stuck elevator. I mean, that's a high-up high if you no-brains can handle that. I'm talking about lying down and staring up at that waffle shit—you know what I'm talking about—that shit up on the ceiling. You ever looked at that shit? I mean really looked at it. Like looked at how if you look at it straight on, straight on, like from lying below it on the elevator floor, from that way the light from the bulbs behind it makes it get a waviness like it was moving or growing even though you know it's just some cheapo plastic waffle shit, but moving, man, even when you are totally still, like I'm telling you I was when I was stuck up between the fiftieth and the forty-ninth floor. And I realized then that they are lying, that plastic and shit like that is really actually alive. That's another thing. Why those floors? Fifty. Forty-nine. Cause that's where the fucking elevator got stuck. Right? Wrong, asshole. It's forty-nine, it's fifty because, don't you know it, the next day at market on close there's going to be an out between the boss and Sligo. He's saying sold at fifty and he's saying sold at forty-nine. And I fucking know it's fifty, not because he's the boss, but because when the elevator got unstuck, it went up to fifty, not down to forty-nine."

"Praise the Lord, that's deep!" Tony P. says.

"Window alert!" shouts Vinnie, doing a little hip thing, and we all take off to the window despite all our knowing that Vinnie is full of shit.

"What about 'Once upon a time,' " says Frank. "Didn't the one of you ever hear about 'Once upon a time'? Shit, don't the one of you got some kind of an education? You got to have a story be like a story, like, 'Once upon a time there was a mighty kingdom. In the kingdom was some tall buildings. These buildings, they was built entirely out of glass and entirely out of steel.' "

"Snore, snore, snore," says Artie, and everyone joins Artie, each with his own particular version of a snore.

"Check this out! Oh baby! Here's a little treat to wake you jerk-offs up," says Artie when one of Ray-ban's clerks comes over to check trades. What alerts attention is this clerk's unmistakable girl assets. My job is to take my sweet time, give the boys a little apprecia-tion time. So when Rayban's girl gets close, I'm already on the phone, pretending that I am seriously busy car-rying on some serious business of the utmost impor-tance. I lift a finger to signal that I'll be off when I can be off. That leaves her to my boys, who get her engaged in some talk that's meant to keep this sweet young thing posed in front of our booth with all of her assets in as much motion as possible.

You don't have to be some kind of reporter for *The New York Times* to see that there is no action on the floor, but I go through the cards real slow like the boss has been piling up the trades.

"You buying or selling?" I say, when I can see perfectly well that I am selling her six lots of augie silver at five and a quarter.

I'm selling her—that's how we talk here, as if all the movement on these cards is our own. Deals, deals, deals. Money in our pocket. All us boys want to be traders. All us boys, all day long, are buying and selling under our breath, and in this way we've made our fortunes ten times over.

"Check trade," I say, and then sit back to get an excellent view of her assets shake back over to Rayban's booth. Her coming over on a slow afternoon was sweet, but it has to be admitted, there's a certain bonus to her leaving.

"I'll take me that as my bedtime story any fucking night," Frank says, and this time the grunts the guys join in with don't sound like snoring the least little bit.

Fred grabs the phone and starts telling us that there is a babe on the line who wants to know if there is any man here with real staying power, a man she says that will give her it straight on through the night. He says she says she's got something special to tell that man; he says she says she's got a story that's going to change his life.

"Sure," Artie says, "for another twenty minutes at

three bucks a minute, it will change all of our goddamn lives."

Then I see, at last, that my turn has come.

So I begin.

"There was once some gentlemen," I say. "There was, once upon a time, some gentlemen once who wagered that the world would never know them as they truly were. These fellows believed no one would get it, their lives, I mean. I mean, these fellows thought that the shit that hit the books was broker shit, not ever clerk-guy shit. Broker shit, they thought, that's bigtime shit, metals and crude and a wife getting her hair done at Bergdorf Goodman while a tootsie's up in the penthouse pulling your rich dick out of Tiffany underpants. Clerk shit, they thought, face it, that's nothing shit, some mother, some lousy car. If you got yourself a choice, these gentlemen thought, between spending your buck on a story about some lousy broker with a fancy car and a wife with a fancy set of tits or a lousy clerk with a lousy car and a wife with her lousy set of tits, these gentlemen declared there would be no choice. These boys went so far as to wager that not only would it not be done but that nobody would ever make a penny sitting down and telling any dumb-ass clerk story.

"A day's wages.

"Then a week's wages.

" 'Fuck a week,' these gentlemen, they said, 'here's a month that nobody's going to do it.'

"A month's wages times seven. You don't have to be any Rockefeller to figure out what's the thing to do. You don't have to be any Shakespeare to say it. You don't have to have a life worth a dime for some smart-ass to make a dime on it. You don't have to be nothing to make something out of a bunch of nothing assholes willing to crap away their lives hoping to become bigger assholes. So now, pals, now, honorable gentlemen, there's only one thing in this historical story left for me to say. Here it is. Ready or not. Vinnie, Fred, Frank, Artie, Tony P., Tony D., and Tommy DeRay, here's your dumb little lives.

"Pay up, you stupid motherfuckers—pay."

SEE THE DOG

I think the kindest part of the story is that I did not remember them waking me up in the middle of the night.

O B U D D H A! Oh, for the man who stands on the hillside perched on one leg. Oh, for the wine and the life of abstention.

The man on one leg looks out over the landscape. What is there to see that would match the attention of living on one leg?

Heaven, cries the Buddha. Just look, there is everything. You've heard it all before—the blade of grass, its complex strategy of taking in water, its greening.

I rise from the subway into April's crazy bloom. Here is the dangle of wisteria; here the yellow kerchief flowering on a woman's head. Here, in a satin baseball jacket, her son's arms are like waxy stems. Here are the carefully potted tulips; here, tight pink jeans cover a teenager's petal thighs. Here the pudgy grapes, the grocer's bouquet of radishes.

My sweetest love, this is my confession—today I love all the junk of the world and somehow love it all equally; resisting nothing, I love neon, synthetics, polyester, magenta rhinestones.

Now the orange letters above the dry cleaner's seem rare as a florist's exotica.

HE WOBBLES a little; you would, too.

He does not think every blade of grass or every curve of hillside is a gorgeous event.

I whistle and I get in trouble with the ladies. Of course, I was whistling at them.

I AM TRYING to concentrate on calamity. I am trying to call back everything I know about the scourge that is history, but I am distracted by the sparrows clamoring and the alert faces of men betting three-card monte.

I will tell you the sorrow of the happy man. It is that I cannot resist knowing who is happier, the little piggy that went to market or the one that stayed home.

See the Dog

Look, I don't have to be Buddha to know that you breathe in and breathe out in either event.

I PUT my brush to the paper and begin. With the curved line, I paint the mountain range; a swift stroke and the waterfall starts down; at the bottom, a wind rises from the green forest and the foaming water rushes in a stream.

See the man, the blunt stroke of his body; he does not wobble in the painting.

Love, pity the happy man—the mountain range is large and the pupil of the eye small. I want to hold it close, within an inch of my eye, but then I do not see its form.

Ah, there. At a distance of, say, seven miles, I enclose the mountain within the square inch of my pupil.

Now I drain the wine cup, play the lute, lay down the picture of scenery, face it with silence, tracking the four borders to wilderness. Here are the cliffs and the peaks. Here the grove; here, stretching out of the mist, is the walkway with its split-rail fence.

Split-rail fence!—someone has been here before me.

How does the happy man pray? He prays like all other men, with the board of directors compiling an agenda in his heart.

* * *

149

IT BEGINS to drizzle, drops connecting on the sidewalk.

I am worried for him, stuck out in the rain, on one determined but unsteady leg. I want to bring him in for this part, towel him dry, promise him that tomorrow will arrive and with it another good, sunny day for perching. How can he not be tempted; the one leg aches and the other is bored and yearns to be set down.

That is the amazement, that the free leg is not content to give up its burden and go along on a free ride.

The rain keeps coming, drops falling in their angled plunge. Umbrellas open; water collects in the cup of the tulip; ladies gather under awnings, waiting like girls at a fireman's ball.

Oh, girls, what could be happier than the happy man in an April shower?

See the dog out in the rain. The dog sniffs and wags its dog tail. See the dog absorbed in the precise situation of its present life.

THE SPARROWS MOVE in a single great flush. One tree to the next. They settle on a branch as if they might stick around for a while, and then they're off. In the center of the sparrows, a tropical shock of green. I look up. Where is the woman leaning halfway out of her window, calling for her pet parakeet to come home? Where is the hand waving a branch of fresh millet?

O God of Happily-Ever-After, hear me out. I am like any other man in this unwieldy garden. Mine is happiness. His is shame.

Abundance, abundance, abundance.

Still, I am dying.

SERVICE SERVIC
SERVI

We were just getting nouveau, *"nuevo,"* Margueurita called it when the boxes arrived. Silver and crystal, mink jackets to summer in storage, chandeliers, and there were French doors to be hung. *"Das ist zu reich,"* squealed Irma when the Oriental was unrolled. Here are the Wedgwood bowls, a security system, a marble-floored foyer where children sprawl playing jacks. Here is Graciela carrying a laundry basket, saying something that sounds like a Spanish curse or a Spanish prayer.

The maids. The maids. The maids. This story, for what it is worth, might have been called "Getting Good Help." And while, obviously, it is not, let me, nevertheless, get all the maids out in the open, to give them, if you will, their due share, their Christmas bonuses, their two weeks' severance pay, their green cards—Immigration willing. Here then are: Graciela; Delia; Leita; Sally; Pilar; Lucha; Lucha's cousin, Luchas; then, what's-her-name? the one Mother swore was Eva Braun; Vilma; Irma; Erlene; Margaret; Margueurita. There are surely more, though these are the only ones whom I can instantly call to mind.

"This introduction of the maids," calls Mother from the dining room, "is typical of your looking at all the wrong things, of your wanting desperately, at all cost, to look so woefully poor."

At dinner, Mother shakes her damsel bell, the brass legs kicking under the brass hoop skirt. The swing door pushes open and here is—oh, who is it? Paviola? Did I mention Paviola?—backing hip-first into the dining room, the silver-service tray offered, always on the proper side and always first to Father. On the dining room walls, there are paintings—a bowl resplendent with fruits, a Loca painting of a barefoot boy. No framed posters in this house. Here is the real thing, spotlighted and in a gilt frame, and, just like all the other paintings, hung throughout this cultured village.

(Of course Mother is right about me with the maids. I would rather serve myself leftovers with whomever on the kitchen side of the swing door than dine here in the clothed and candlelighted dining room.)

"S'il vous plaît," calls Mother, "take your guilt and give us all a break."

* * *

PLEASE, let me now jump ahead, out the front door, past Enrico and Dante clipping the shrubs, to show you the SERVIC sign, that is SERVICE minus the *E* that Mother's Cadillac tore off. This is the SERVIC sign that points down the driveway to the back door, though unfortunately, this SERVIC door brings us full circle back, all too quickly, particularly to Delia, or generally back to maids.

It was, Mother claims, the power steering that brought the Cadillac beyond the ninety degrees and into the arm of the darky jockey (yes, the very kind you imagine—monkey-sized, in riding silks, lamp in one hand. They must be against the law by now), temporarily taking down the sign and permanently taking off the *E*. The Caddy was not harmed, just a little gold paint from one of the blackamoor's buttons scratched into the fender.

It was only later that Mother's conviction flowered, if conviction can be considered a thing to have a pollination, a germination, a bud to be nipped or bloomed. Imagine Mother's ire coming to the just-created SERVIC door, seeing Delia polishing the silver serving tray, the three partitions—meat, vegetable, and potato—gleaming, ready for food, and in Mother's hand the local paper with a full inventory of stolen goods from the heist at 45 White Birch Lane, new maid MIA.

Did it matter that said housekeeper was Jamaican and Delia was Georgia-bred right back to the ball-and-chain boat?

"It is so easy to ridicule," calls Mother from the dining room, "but answer me this. Does Father work night and day so that we should just open the door and hand out our possessions like holiday candy?"

ROOM TO ROOM, let us go now. No tricks and all treats! Let us peer into the loot bag filled with Father's night-and-day money, now in the form of Mother's Royal Copenhagen china, statuettes from the pastoral, the boy milking his cow, the woman with her bouquet of balloons, the weeping mermaid on her craggy rock. Spode, yes, there is Spode. Waterford. Rosenthal. Baccarat. And here is more Royal Copenhagen: ashtrays, vases, water pitchers, ice buckets, just to slake your thirst for Danes. I will not mention the silver, because what thief, especially a maid who has borne the weight of the silver tray or the serving dish, what clever thief is going to load up on these hefty goodies and hope for a speedy getaway?

And then there are things I have sworn to Mother I would not mention, but which reside in a certain combination safe (25-9-13) behind a certain painting of a kneeling Spanish girl.

SERVIC door be damned!—there goes Delia right out the front door, past the children sprawled on the marble-floored foyer, jacks lined up for fancies, out the front door with a suitcase that is light enough to keep her indignation buoyant, Mother already on the phone checking a new girl's references and the children now taking the attic stairs two at a time to search the cleared-out dresser for a bobby pin, matches, a love letter wedged in a drawer runner, some little anything that the girl has left behind.

FOR THE READER'S clarification, the security system is dipartite. Part one is the red light glowing in the hall closet. Open a door, crack a window for air or for entrée and the police station switchboard will light and *brrrng* and otherwise indicate a location of possible perturbation. If it is an accident—just listen to all the false alarms ringing through this town— you must give your password. I, for your edification, would say (against Mother's wishes) that ours is C.L.A.S.S.Y.1.2.3.

NEXT COMES part two. Part two is the panic button. This backup, which (heaven forbid!) no maid is shown, but which each must surely discover in the course of a thorough cleaning, is the "oh my God, the black man's inside" button by Mother's bed. No phone call. No password. In three minutes, they enter, guns drawn and cocked, Paviola caught with the drapery attachment sucking at the chintz window treatment.

"Better safe than poor," warns Mother from the dining room.

MOTHER CLAIMED it was all sixth sense.

With this girl, truth was revealed in an insomniac's vision and a crack-of-dawn cross-check in the town library, then a bursting seventh sense that took the driveway turn prepared for historic revelation and righteously tore the C off the SERVIC sign.

Room to room to room, Mother followed her Eva Braun. Mother waited for a false move, a mistress's telltale toss of hair. Eva Braun kept her hair suspiciously in a net. Mother ordered that at all meals Sabbath candles would be lit. Prayers were said over bologna and mayonnaise sandwiches. The children were instructed, even the girls, to don prayer caps.

By day, Mother sent the fräulein to remote corners of the basement with strict instructions to make cement floors sparkle. The boiler was to shine. The heating unit was scraped and desludged. Mother instructed Ms. Braun to scrub the toilets twice a day.

During a lightning storm, Mother sent Mistress Braun to the roof to pull leaves from the gutters.

Calls were placed to Washington.

At the week's end, when the Little Führerette slammed the SERVI door behind her, Mother said that justice had prevailed.

"You laugh now, my darling daughter," Mother

shouts from the dining room. "But did anyone of consequence ever verify the body?"

"ENOUGH IS enough!" screams Mother from the dining room. "This story has gotten entirely out of hand. Why don't you, Little Miss Equality, march everybody right up to your room and continue your brilliant exposé of the nouveau riche. You want to talk tribulation of maids, let's talk about your room, Little Miss Proletariat. Just who is changing your sheets? You want to talk tchotchkes . . . well, let's have a peek, dearie. Shelves of crystal—geodes, rare iolite from Tanzania, Brazilian hocus-pocus crystal—and figures— African, Australian, South Bronxian fertility carvings, Navajo fetish dolls and fetid fruit-dye weavings—all I can say, mademoiselle, is at least the Royal Copenhagen is dishwasher-safe. And, by the way, exactly who is washing and pressing all those embroidered Guatemalan blouses sold to you by some I-am-in-solidarity-with-the-peoples-of-the-world type for a mere fifty, a mere one hundred socially concerned dollars?"

"But, please," says Mother, sipping pinkie up from her teacup, "don't let me put a damper on your glorious revolution."

WHICH BRINGS us to Katerina.
Katerina arrived at the front door in her own uni-

form, starched and bowed in the back. Her legs were delicate, her hands creamed. Katerina made a list of supplies for Mother: waxes from England, fruitwood polish from Provence, an Austrian cloth for Austrian glass, and a New Zealand sheepskin for polishing we did not know what. Katerina set the Rosenthal for everyday use. She turned over silver to check for hallmarks. At dinner, there was a parade of flatware—dessert, salad, meat, and fish fork with corresponding knives flanking the service plate; butter knives saluting on butter plates—a skyline of goblets for water and wine. Katerina served in black linen piped in cream-colored silk, her hair rolled stylishly in a bun.

Then one night, we saw the ring.

Five, seven, perhaps ten carats' worth of diamond, according to Mother. No occlusions. No yellow. It was an old mine diamond. We forgot to worry about the order of forks.

"Seconds, madam," said Katerina, the jewel flashing close to Mother.

Mother whispered, "I'm not hungry."

Katerina wore the diamond only at dinner. But it did not matter. We had seen it. It was there, a twinkle, a phantom sparkle, when Katerina was on her knees, elbow-deep in ammonia or perched on a step stool dusting chandeliers. When Katerina went to take out the garbage, Mother said, "No, no, let me."

First a "No, no, let me," then a "Please, let me," then it is off with the Gucci, off with the Cacharel; here now is Mother in a faded muumuu, helping

Katerina make beds. They are polishing silver. They are talking family trees. They are off to the beauty salon. And here they come in the Cadillac, coiffed and shellacked, running down the grinning jockey, just one riding boot left (sans corpus) in the ground. At dinner, the swing door ajar, Katerina is seated, glittering by Mother's side.

ALERT! ALERT! Sound the alarm!

Just like that, the ring was gone. The police questioned us in separate rooms.

Vacuum bags were opened. Drains were checked.

The captain held Katerina's creamed hand. He draped his captain's jacket over her slender, heaving shoulders. He eyed Mother suspiciously.

You think, Mother.

Of course.

Mother plotting.

Mother sneaking up the back hall stairs, filching the sparkling rock while the fair Katerina sleeps without a grunt. Down the stairs and 25—two turns right—9—one turn left—13, and, voilà, Mother is saying, "What ring is that, Captain? Yes, yes, Captain, I vaguely remember a ring."

Soon enough, you think, she will reveal her crime, caught sporting that beauty, golfing at the country club with a knockout gem that—hands down—outdazzles all the knockoffs.

Oh, Captain, you, think again.

* * *

IT IS LONG after the children have zip, zip, zipped up their jacks and suitcases. We have bolted out doors—front and SERVI—off to campgrounds and communes with disregarded job wheels, off to yard sales and pawnshops. We are up elevators to one-bed-rooms. With a nod to the doorman and the concierge, I go up, up, and up to my family home, where my girl, Shirley, comes Thursdays.

They are there, the two of them, still at the dining room table.

Windows, laundry, she's a gem.

"My," she says. "My, my, that, Missus, is surely something."

I say, "Yes, Shirley, you are right. It is old. Well, my God, it has been in our family for—my God, I couldn't possibly even say—oh, my God, I guess it has been around—on one hand or another—for generations."

MENDER OF THE HOUSE AND OF OTHER MODEST OBJECTS

*M*orning is her block of porch light, where Nana says it is so bright she must close her eyes to clearly see the hole to thread the needle. Grandpa is a painting just outside the porch-room door. To look at me, I am, Nana tells me, her sister, dead, her Rosha. Any time of day, shut eye and shaking hand, Nana does not miss the needle. Handling cloth, she says, "There are years still in this."

As for Grandpa, he is a young man in a frame hanging crooked on the wall.

We are all of us in this house dressed by Nana's hand.

By Nana's hand, a dress is a dress is a shirt is a skirt are shorts and pants, Nana says, are the thing that a scratcher like me needs for the buggy kind of day this is.

This day outside comes in through the mesh of Nana's porch.

My pants are a checkered dress split and pinned and ready to be tried on, with Grandpa hanging slanted on the wall. Grandpa wears a suit of blue. My pants are a blue-checked dress. Nana's teeth rest on a plate on the blue sewing tray.

"Hold still," says Nana, and pricks me, basting up my leg, her mouth a sucked-in flower nettled full of pins.

NANA IS early coming down to her porch. But I have been up since earlier, peeking through the door crack to watch her washing. I see her with the towel and see how it is lovelier this way, seeing, at once, only parts of her, the flat, hanged dangle of a breast, a white hand steadying its burden on the white tile. I see Nana's legs, girlish at the ankles, see the folds of stomach and the dark thread down to where the water beads. I see the drift of talcum, the rub of lotion, the splash of toilet water, and patted dry, Nana leans over, putting herself into a brassiere, stepping into underpants. I see Nana's teeth balanced on the tub's lit rim. And Nana, now dressed and teethed, says, and always so suddenly, "Get my scissors."

Now it is my turn now to hold the scissors, sitting with my back to Nana, who sits, I know without looking, sloped back on the covered toilet. Her foot is in my lap. Her toenails are thick, ridged, crested yellow like bone close to where they ridge down under the skin. The skin is pumiced smooth with bony calluses on her such thin-boned feet.

"Not such a hurry," says Nana, and "Not so sloppy," says Nana, touching her fingers to her toes, saying, "Here and here," and "I would do it fine myself but for the vision, the vision," and saying, finally, "Give me them back!" her body curling even farther over and her foot yanked up into her own lap.

BY HAND, by treadle, by motor, there is always an eyed needle to be threaded. And now, needle in hand, Nana's head nods, and I watch her jerk and snort, and when her head falls to the side where the sun strikes her eyes, she wakes.

"Rosha," she says, "hurry with your lace and hooks; Mother is waiting."

Nana says Grandpa is Joseph back from Egypt come up the front path to court, not Nana, but this younger sister, this Rosha—now me—who says, "Sure, Nana. Anything you say."

What Nana says she sees is Joseph wrapping me in his coat and leading me to the river. She sees her father's garden and us in the distance, with Joseph's coat a fruited bough spread over us. Nana, standing at the door, thinks she can smell the fever far off and drifting near on this house. What is sown by the bank, by the splash of carried water, by the stinger of a carrier bug is what sweep of fever Nana tries to wrest from her sister with hot glasses. Joseph's coat is brushed and burned far from the garden. But the far-off fever is stronger even than the hand of my Nana, which, shaking or still, is still stronger even than the heart of Joseph.

I am Rosha, betrothed, and laid down in a lace dress, and my beloved wakes under the coverlet of a practical wife.

My sister mends his suits, sews him a new coat, with a crust of bread tacked into the breast pocket.

By summer, the river is flaking clay and stalks.

I AM a picture on their dresser table.

NANA PICKS UP with her needle when she starts from a doze, and, even now, I have counted her thirty stitches to the minute. Nana's dress is medaled with pins—straight and safety. Her teeth are bones on the sewing table. I have seen my Nana pull a fever from her own chest like a stray hair off a chin; and where she could not reach to, I have tilted her head back into the light and tweezed thin her random beard.

Joseph is Grandpa, on a wall, wearing the red curls of a groom's carnation.

My Nana calls out to me as her sister, and when I go to shake her, she cries, "You better watch out for me!"

Nana stays down in her chair even after the room has thinned of daylight. By day-by-day, through night, she will still be at it, her needle twisting in the air, mending whatever she can get at.

Washing it.

Cutting it back.

Doing whatever must be done.

Her hands all over it, so that—whatever it is—it will not take her unprepared.

A NOTE ABOUT THE AUTHOR

Victoria Redel was educated at Dartmouth College and Columbia University. She teaches and lives in New York City.

A NOTE ON THE TYPE

The text of this book was set in Sabon, a type face designed by Jan Tschichold (1902–1974), the well-known German typographer. Because it was designed in Frankfurt, Sabon was named for the famous Frankfurt type founder Jacques Sabon, who died in 1580 while manager of the Egenolff foundry.

Based loosely on the original designs of Claude Garamond (c. 1480–1561), Sabon is unique in that it was explicitly designed for hot-metal composition on both the Monotype and Linotype machines as well as for film composition.

Composed, printed, and bound by
Haddon Craftsmen,
Scranton, Pennsylvania
Designed by Cassandra J. Pappas